DEATH ON

DUVAL ST.

A Perry Savant Novel

HERB SENNETT

For information about the publisher:
    CIF Publications
    1565 Woodbridge Lakes Circle
    West Palm Beach, FL 33406
    www.cifpublications.com

For information about the author:
    www.novelsbyherb.com
    www.herbsennett.com
    herb@herbsennett.com

Text edited by Roger Colby & Herb Sennett
Book printer: CreateSpace, an Amazon Company
Book Cover design by Herbert Sennett

ISBN 13: 978-0-9970231-1-4
ISBN 10: 0997023112
First Edition: November 2015

10 9 8 7 6 5 4 3 2

For Cristie

Acknowledgements

I WISH TO THANK the people who had a part in helping make this book possible. First I have dedicated this book to the person who read the first draft of this idea and told me that I definitely needed to get this story published.

The people who helped to make this book into what it is today include Paul S. Levine, who encouraged me to work on the story to make it the best it can be. I also wish to thank my friend, Daniel Valencia who listened to me describe the story idea and told me it should be made into a novel. And I also thank the many people who suffered long listening to me talk through so many of the ideas I had.

Most of all, I wish to thank my editor Roger Colby who patiently walked through several of the last drafts carefully and meticulously showing me where I could improve my writing and the story. For the many hours he spent giving me encouragement to continue, I will forever be grateful. Oh, and he'll be looking at the final drafts of the next novel in the ongoing saga of Perry Savant, **Death on A1A**.

Finally, I am grateful to have such a wonderful, loving family who care enough to sit and listen to me blabber on about my story ideas. I can never thank them enough. My wife, Beverly; my son, Alan; my daughter-in-law, Cindy; my daughter, Cristie; her boyfriend, Daniel; and of so much importance, my grandson, Eliot, who makes my whole world seem worthwhile.

To my Christian friends around the world, I wish to say that I hope the message in this book is clear. I have read and think I understand the message that Jesus brought to us: a message of loving acceptance of human beings just as they are. Only then do we earn the right to share the gospel message.

If Jesus Christ was willing to give his life to make our lives worthwhile, then we have a responsibility to show that kind of love through our lives to all those around us. Our job is to show love. God's job is to do the judging. A thought to ponder.

One

I'M A WRITER, NOT A DETECTIVE. But thinking that I could be is how I made the mistake of overestimating my own skills and talent.

One of my best friends had been murdered with thousands of people standing nearby. And yet, there were no witnesses. I only wanted to help the police and another friend, a private investigator, in finding the killer.

But, it seems that my arrogance got in the way of my common sense. And that's how I nearly lost my life.

‡ ‡ ‡

I THINK IT WAS the third of February when it all started; my eyes popped open before dawn. I experienced a feeling of dread, a thickness in the air; it felt like something that gets stuck to your skin. And I felt a dreadful foreboding as if I was about to receive a horrendous phone call or perhaps the dreaded knock on the door.

Did I know anything in particular other than I had an aching in my stomach and my heart beat heavy in my chest? No. I knew nothing except that deep aching inside that says to you, "Something terrible is about to happen."

Well, actually, I had been under extra pressure over the past month or so. The income from my books had dropped about ten percent, and my publisher called a couple of months earlier wanting a full update on the progress of the next two books I was scheduled to finish. In a sense I felt it was time to go out and get a real job and earn a salary. Perhaps if I were married, my wife would be giving me fits. I guess I had plenty of reason to worry.

But, since I'm a pessimistic person by nature, I simply shook it off because, well, I already had too much to worry about. Besides, I had work that needed to get done during the day. I had no extra time for useless worry. I mean, ten years ago I believed that turning thirty would mean that my life was completely over, done, caput.

Now I am thirty-six and, let's just say, I'm still kicking. Besides, I worry about everything anyway, so I added the emotion of foreboding to the long list I carry with me every day just in case I need something to obsess on.

I looked at myself in the mirror noticing the little lines beginning to cut the skin around my eyes and at the edges of my lips. I splashed water on my face and proceeded to do my morning ritual: shave, shower, and then sit on the throne for ten minutes thinking about the day ahead of me.

After eating a bowl of cereal at the table in my small kitchen, I carried a cup of coffee with me and sat down at my writing table next to the open window that looked out onto Eaton Street. I called my desk a writing table since that's about the only thing I do at it. There was plenty of room on the 36" by 60" top. It was built for someone who needed a smooth surface to write on. I use a computer to write. The irony did not escape me.

I'd blown over a thousand bucks a month on this apartment that took the ground floor of a small, two-story twenties-era house. I was happy to pay that because it was located a half block from Duval Street, the center of most of the action in this small town of Key West.

A porch extended the length of the front by about a foot on either side and faced the south. The second floor was fronted with a balcony giving the front porch a comfortable shade in the hot afternoons. It also partially shaded the morning sun soon after sunrise.

The door on the left of the building led to an apartment on the second floor. The door to the right led to my apartment which occupied the whole first floor. I usually tell people that fact because it makes the apartment sound bigger than it really is.

I loved Key West from the first time my family brought me here on vacation more than twenty years ago. Therefore, I found it quite easy to move here when I made the transition from journalist to novelist. This apartment offered a comfortable place to call home with its four rooms including a front room where I could work, a kitchen, a large bedroom with a bathroom off to the side.

And there's that smaller "extra room" that is hardly big enough to store eight or ten boxes and my two pieces of luggage. At first glance, I thought it was a closet; but there were no shelves or racks to hang things on. It was, well, empty.

The moment I first walked into the house, I could see that it was built to accommodate a second floor apartment to rent out while the owners lived on the bottom floor, or vice versa. I rented the first level from the owner who lived in Chicago after he spent an hour telling me how he had inherited it from his uncle. Or was it his father?

I love living just off Duval Street since that's where most of the social and tourist action happens in this small town at the southern end of US Highway One. All sorts of events occur on this main north/south thoroughfare where nearly two hundred businesses of various types and sizes are scattered about.

I sat at my computer on this clear day looking at the breaking light of the sunrise to the east. The few people up at that hour walked by and couldn't help but notice me sitting at my desk pounding away on the keyboard. Nosy tourists walking by may have thought I was probably a pervert surfing the net because of my habit of sitting in a pair of shorts and no shirt.

But, in reality, I was banging out the next "great American novel." At least I hoped the one I was working on would be the one that would make me rich. Today I was praying it would be true.

Most of the permanent residents around here know of

my work and stop to see how the writing is going. I like to pretend that I'm busy but always happy to take time away from my writing to talk about my next novels0. Most of the time I'm just happy to do anything but pound out meaningless drivel as I pretend to write.

Sometimes when the air is crisp I take my laptop out to the porch and sit in a large, old rattan rocking chair that some people say had to be at least a hundred years old. Actually I find solace and inspiration living in this small town where the people know one another. The atmosphere helps me feel relaxed enough to free my imagination.

Unfortunately, my imagination would often stop at the open gate of my mind afraid to fly. You see, at the time of this story, I was suffering with a serious case of writer's block. And this had been going on for nearly three months.

People passing by wave or say "hello." I always make it a point to acknowledge them and act like I'm getting back to the business of writing. Actually I learned to be disciplined enough never to lose my place or thoughts when disturbed. Even when in the throes of writer's block, I believe that a smile and a nod helps to maintain a good rapport with the neighbors, most of whom buy my books, and later stop by and ask me to autograph it.

While in college, I learned the habit of writing no less than ten pages per day whether I kept them or not. My writing teacher at Emerson College often said, "Even if you end up throwing those pages away, just make sure you are writing. Just like any skill, use it or lose it."

So, every morning I write something, never flagging on the commitment I made to Professor White to do what he told me to do. I rise at six and write from seven until one in the afternoon. Then I take a break for lunch.

By the way, I'm that person who hates to do house work. And I despise cooking for myself. So everyday instead of fixing something to eat, I walk down to the Monument Street Café located at the corner of Whitehead and Petronia in the middle of Bahama Village around lunch time. There I eat, talk with patrons, and relax before getting back to my writing.

The great thing about living in Key West's Old Town is that everything you may need is within walking distance. So, I enjoyed exercising by walking the seven blocks to the restaurant. Sometimes I ride my scooter, depending on whether or not I had other errands to run. Sometimes I pack my laptop in the baggage container under the seat and arrive at the café by eight for breakfast and sit most of the day typing and eating.

After lunch on this particular February day, I rode my scooter to the Key West Public Library to research the locations of several of the sunken wrecked eighteenth-century ships in the region. I needed this research to add details to enhance the believability of the story I was working on. I was hoping that in reviewing the maps, charts, records, and other materials I would be inspired and break out of this brain freeze I was experiencing.

As I entered the Florida History Room, the archivist nodded to me and said, "Good afternoon, Mr. Morrison. You want those same charts again, or do I need to get some others?"

"If you don't mind, just the ones I had out the other day.

And, Carl, please call me Jay."

"I just don't feel right, you know. I mean I was raised to call folks by their last name, you know. And besides, you being a famous author and all."

"I know. I love that about you."

"I'll fetch those charts for you, Mr., er, uh, James."

I smiled as I watched him walk back into the storage area to retrieve the numerous charts I had worked on earlier. Many had marks on them indicating the confirmed and suspected sites of sunken ships.

At about two that afternoon, I was deep in concentration making notations on an old yellow note pad as I studied the charts and maps. I felt the cell phone buzzing in my pocket. Pulling it out and checking the screen I saw that it was my agent Holly Beard calling from her New York office.

"Hold on a moment, Holly," I said as I moved through the library passing the main desk on my way out onto Fleming Street.

"Sorry, I was in the library. What's up? Calling to check on me, seeing if I'm writing?"

"Of course I am. Did you expect anything less?" she said, laughing.

"Of course not."

"So, how's the project coming?"

"Fine. Knee deep in old, dusty charts of the Florida Straits."

"Good."

I Paused.

"Okay, Holly. What's up?"

"Nothing, darling. I just like to keep tabs on my favorite

writers."

"Holly, dear, I know you too well. What's wrong?"

"Nothing's wrong, Jay, really. Just wanted to call to be sure you're going to be in town Friday."

"Yeah, and?"

"I decided I need to come spend a little time with my favorite novelist."

"Holly, we've known each other too long. What's up? Really."

"Honey, it's just too damn cold here in New York City. Besides I need an excuse to take a vacation without, you know, using vacation time. So, I'm coming to Key West; and since I'll be spending time with you--"

"You can take the trip expenses off your income taxes.

"Am I that transparent?"

"You need me to pick you up at the airport?"

"Not if you're going to meet me on that motorized skateboard," she said.

"Okay, just grab a cab. I'll meet you at the Monument Street Café."

"Your compassion underwhelms me."

"Hey. You're the one who hates my scooter."

"I should be in around 2:30," she said with that I'm all business tone she gets when she was tired of sparring. "I've got reservations at the La Concha. I fly back Monday at 1:20 p.m."

"Good. We'll have a chance to visit."

"I expect you to be your normal charming self."

"Best behavior, darling. I promise."

"See you Friday," she said and hung up.

I put the phone back in my pocket and wondered just what was going on. She's up to something, I thought as I sat down on the bench near the front entrance taking a moment to enjoy the shade and light breeze blowing from off the gulf. Suddenly I felt a deep painful churning in my stomach just like I had when I woke up.

Damn! I thought. She's going to try to pressure me into writing something new. Or she's going tell me the publisher has decided to drop me because my book sales are in the tank.

I shook my head and thought, I can't worry about this until she brings it up this weekend.

For a moment, my mind drifted back to when we first met in New York City. I was in a meeting with Larry Carmichael, Editorial Chief for Hollister Publishing, along with three of the company's attorneys. We were in the middle of finalizing the contract for my first three novels. Carmichael handed me a small piece of paper with a name and address on it.

He was recommending Holly Beard, a literary agent located a few buildings down the street.

One of the attorneys pointed at the paper and said, "Mr. Hollister has already called and made arrangements for this agent to represent you. Just call the number and she'll take you on as a client."

"Sight unseen?" I asked.

From his chair at the end of the long conference table where we were sitting, Mr. Hollister stood up and walked to where I was seated and said, "She's one of the best in the country, young man. If you're not referred to her, she won't even talk to you. Feel lucky; this is a great opportunity. Besides, she a friend and she'll help me hold on to you."

Not being a total idiot, I called her immediately after the meeting was over and signed a contract with her that afternoon. And just like that, my professional writing career was launched.

Wait, I thought. If Holly wants to press me on writing something different; well, I'll just have to do it. If she wants to tell me personally that I'm being dropped, I'll just get another publisher. I've faced worse in my life. I can face this.

So, my instincts had been correct at the outset of this day. Something did happen, something significant. And yet, I still had no idea what. I stiffened and thought, if my agent and my publisher want things to change, I'll just have deal with it.

Slapping my knees, I stood up and walked back into the library and into the Florida History Room. As I reached for my magnifying glass, I gave a silent sigh, picked up the old charts, and got back to work on my research.

TWO

Friday, February Sixth

I HAD JUST FINISHED a late lunch when Holly Beard
walked into the Monument Street Café. The building was
not very large, with room for only fifteen tables inside and
ten on the large patio out back. Most people would eat
inside during the day. At night the tables outside filled very
quickly after which people would stand in line to get a table.

There were five other tables located on the sidewalk
along Whitehead Street, but most people found it
uncomfortable trying to eat next to such a busy traffic zone.

The building was a converted house built in the 1890's.
The owners of the restaurant stretched old parachutes
between the several trees in the back yard, creating a
comfortable, shady atmosphere for dining day and night.

But usually people would eat on the patio later in the afternoon or during the winter months when the air was crisp but not cold. On those days the patio filled fast.

When Holly walked in, the people in the dining room turned to look at her. She was tall with a gracefulness that I can only describe as classy. It seemed to make her forty-five years seem like thirty. Every time she visited me, I found myself staring at her, one of those statuesque women who are painfully unaware of how pretty they are.

A contented divorcé, Holly fought her way through two bad marriages then gave up on that particular pursuit. She decided to dedicate herself to her career as more rewarding than a relationship with a man. Now with her daughter in her first year at Vassar, she was free to take her career to the next level with greater gusto and the hopes of much greater returns.

I always respected the fact that Holly possesses great confidence in herself and her skills. Having been in publishing for more than twenty-five years, she knew the business and just about everyone in it in New York City. She also knew a few key people in Los Angeles whom she could contact whenever she felt she had a novel that needed to be shopped around at the studios for a possible film adaptation.

Although she made an excellent salary, the bonus money she got from selling the movie rights for one of her client's books was often invested to insure her personal retirement. She also planned to have money to leave her daughter who made the transition to an absentee father quite well.

As Holly weaved her way through the tables, she

seemed to be drawn to several regulars sitting at the bar to her right. She even waved to the bartender who nodded his head in acknowledgement with a look of embarrassment. I guess he didn't remember her since it had been a year since she had spent that two weeks of sheer joy and relaxation in Key West. But she acknowledged him anyway; she had that kind of personality.

She pushed her way through the empty tables until she was standing across from me. I didn't look up. I just pounded away on another paragraph I would probably delete anyway. Of course I was pretending I didn't see her come in. She realized the game she was supposed to play and sat down.

She waited for a moment then spoke in a quiet voice, "You seem fully engaged in your novel."

I stopped typing. I looked up, my face stern. "Oh. Hi, Holly; I didn't notice you come in."

Unable to stop myself, I broke into a smile.

"Jay, you're impossible."

"But you love me anyway."

"You make me too much money to hate you."

"Speaking of money, how's Hollister doing?"

"Hollister's fine."

"He ought to be. I've helped make him a millionaire."

"Darling, Hollister was a multi-millionaire long before he signed you on as one of his authors. His millions made it possible for him to take a gamble on you."

"It paid off. You want to order something?"

As she nodded, I signaled for the waitress to come over to the table.

"It's sure nice out."

"It's just like this nearly every day of the year, Holly. You know that."

The waitress approached and Holly ordered a veggie burger and a salad with fat free ranch dressing.

I looked at her and shook my head as the waitress walked away. "Still eating like a bird."

"When I'm cold I just have to eat all the time. So, when I come south I don't want to eat. I guess that's why I make excuses for coming down here so much. Besides, Key West is a nice reprieve from the nasty weather in the city."

"Bad winter?"

"I don't believe in that groundhog crap. They say we're in for at least another six weeks of winter again this year; same as last year. I think I'm ready to go up there and shoot that little hairy rat."

"I remember those long winters."

She stared hard at me. I glanced away as if ashamed at what I had said.

"Oh, that's right. You spent your childhood upstate."

"Don't forget the two miserable years in Boston. God! It was cold."

"Those years in Potsdam after college didn't help either. Did they?"

"At least they helped me mature as a writer. So, I have no bad feelings about Potsdam at all.

Holly began to smile as if she realized that I was staring at her as she sat there looking out the window onto Whitehead Street. The waitress brought her order and set it down.

"Can I get you anything else?"

Holly shook her head and the waitress walked away. Holly took a big bite out of her burger.

"Mm this is good," she slurred, with her mouth full as a little bit of veggie oil seeped out around the corners of her mouth.

I tried not to but I just had to chuckle a bit, covering my mouth with my hand. Both of us let go and laughed, Holly spitting part of her food out as she grabbed for a napkin.

After a moment or two, she poured some dressing on her salad and began to eat as I stared out the window. We sat in silence for several minutes as Holly ate.

After finishing, she spoke.

"So, are you ready to tell me what this new novel is going to be about?"

I stared at her for a second, hoping she couldn't read the worry painted on my face. It seemed she knew I was wondering what her trip was all about. But, I decided to simply play along until she was ready to tell me.

"It's the story of how the Spanish Galleon Santa Martha found its way to the Florida Straits and met up with pirates that sunk her just off the coast of the Dry Tortugas."

I had known Holly long enough that I knew she often tried to sound enthusiastic when uninterested in the topic at hand. But I knew she was failing when she said, "Sounds fascinating."

"Yeah," I said after a brief pause, my eyes darting away. "It'll sell 'cause people have nothing better to do than to buy my novels and sit around and read this mindless drivel."

"Why do you write it?"

"Hollister pays me an excellent royalty on the sales of my books, even after you take your ten percent. I guess I'm getting used to having a nice bank account."

Holly finished her last bite, called the waitress for her check.

"Put his tab on my bill, too." The waitress nodded and walked away.

"You didn't have to do that."

"I know. But I feel better when I do. Look, since I'll be here over the weekend, just call if you want to get together."

She placed two twenties on the table and stood to leave. "I'll tell you what. Why don't we meet for breakfast on Monday? That way you won't feel obligated to call me and try to be sociable. We'll talk about a few things before I fly out. Okay? And then I can write off this trip as a business expense."

I stood and reached out my hand. Holly shook it.

"Until Monday," I said.

Holly nodded, turned, and walked out of the restaurant.

I sat back down and just looked at her as she crossed the room and left through the front entrance. All the while I found myself staring at her. I even continued to watch as she left and walked down Whitehead toward Angela Street where she turned to the right and out of my sight. I just sat there pondering our conversation and finally decided to turn my attention back to the novel.

I typed for about an hour when I just stopped, pushed back away from the keyboard realizing that this heroine I was writing was just like Holly. So, I scrolled back to the beginning of the novel and read from there. I turned about twenty pages and shouted out loud, "Damn!"

People all around the restaurant stopped talking and turned around to look at me. All I could do was just sit there, my face flushed with embarrassment. Sometimes when I write, I zone out so much that I forget where I am and what is happening around me.

It was a strange and pointed talent which gave me the ability to focus my attention so that I churn out at least two novels every year almost one hundred percent without mistakes. But it was that same ability that often caused me trouble, you know, missed phone calls, people talking and waving at me since I seemed to be ignoring them, and often causing a bit of a situation in my favorite restaurant.

"Sorry," I said to no one in particular.

Everyone turned back to what they were doing. I closed the writing program on the computer, went to the file and deleted the novel. I was not about to write a novel with Holly Beard in it. I packed the computer in its case, left a ten spot on the table for the waitress, and walked out of the restaurant.

‡   ‡   ‡

MONDAY MORNING, Holly walked into the restaurant and spotted me sitting in my usual spot. This time I was eating breakfast instead of typing away on the computer. She approached and sat across from me at the table. The waitress was there as if appearing from nowhere and took her order for a short stack with sugar-free syrup. I looked at her and said, "Okay, so what was the trip down here really about?"

"You don't beat around the bush like you used to."

For a couple of seconds, I think I may have appeared to be caught off guard. I recovered and said, "No. I guess I've gotten too old to play stupid games."

"Okay, Jay, here it is. Mr. Hollister is very pleased with your last two novels. Stories about the early development of Key West, pirate ships, fascinating characters, and dramatic rescues of women in distress have sold well."

"I appreciate Hollister publishing my books."

Holly cleared her throat and continued, "And he hopes you're satisfied with the royalties."

"Uh, more than happy."

A rather long and uncomfortable pause ensued.

Holly broke the silence with, "But--"

"But, what?"

"Um, he was wondering if maybe you could do something a little more, well, more up to date and, well, exciting. You know?"

"More exciting? Like what?"

"Well, like a murder mystery or something dealing with international intrigue. Like maybe a thriller."

"I write historical novels about the Florida Keys. And I'm good at it."

"Of course you are. We all know that. But, well, Mr. Hollister and his partners were wondering if you might like to write something thrilling about Key West today."

I didn't know what to say, so I just muttered, "Key West today?"

"Yes."

"Key West today. I'm not sure; I mean; well, nothing exciting ever happens in Key West."

Just then, Brian Silver approached with a flair that befit his position as a major entertainer in Key West. He was dressed in an expensive suit with a bright pink shirt and matching tie. But, around his neck, he was wearing a long, oversized bright red scarf that drug on the floor. He would swing it so that it would hit people in a flirting way.

With a flair for the dramatic, Brian turned around with a whirl and looked into Holly's eyes and said, "Hello, Jay. And who is this beautiful creature? You haven't moved in a different direction, have you?"

"Oh, please, Brian. This is my literary agent, Holly Beard."

Brian moved closer to her, speaking in a soft and tender voice as he said, "I'm Crystal Meth, darling. I'm so glad to meet you."

Among the few things that bothered me about Brian was his insistence upon always being on stage. So I quickly butted in with, "Holly Beard, meet Brian Silver. His stage name is Crystal Meth."

"Is that really your stage name?" Holly said, covering a smile with her hand and looking at me.

"He's a performer, you know, a drag queen?" I continued.

"Of course you are! Nice to meet you, Crystal."

With a gleam in his eye, Brian retorted, "At least you're more accommodating and considerate than some people I know."

"Brian, you know how much I love and appreciate you,

but the act doesn't belong on the streets."

Brian scowled, "Some people wouldn't recognize great talent if it slapped them on the ass."

He slung the scarf so that it slapped me across the face and drifted to another part of the cafe to engage a table with a group of men.

"Jay?" Holly said fully engaged and amused.

"Brian and I go way back to when he first arrived."

"Did he come here because he was gay?"

"Heavens no; Brian's not gay. He just pretends to be."

"What?"

"He's a talented entertainer, a female impersonator, but he thinks he has to be this Crystal Meth character in public in order to sustain the popularity of his stage act."

"What's his background?"

"Brian became an institution in the Key West entertainment scene when he premiered his performance as Jennifer Lopez in a local drag show five years ago. Brian was able to recreate Lopez in such a way that few people can tell the difference between his performance and the real person."

"He's that good?"

"Yes he is. He even followed up that act with a rendition of Christina Aguilera that scared the people at the concert. Many of them asked aloud if she had actually shown up and substituted for this newcomer as sort of joke."

"That's interesting."

"Brian is a master at impersonating famous Latin women. But he wasn't finished. We got a lot of encouragement from Ruthie Mae Jean, she's the owner of a gay show bar down the street, who discovered him in a small bar in Miami. Well, he created a version of Barbara Streisand that brought people to their feet in tears within seconds after he premiered his act at the Ta-Da Club. That was a moment that few, if any, Key West residents will ever forget."

Holly gave those words a moment of thought and said, "Well, He sure seemed gay to me. I mean, I was fooled."

"That's what he wants people to think. You know, never judge a book by its cover?"

"Uh--"

"Holly, looks are deceiving, especially in Key West."

"You're correct," she replied. Then with a deep breath she continued, "So, what about Hollister's suggestion?"

I paused staring at my empty plate. I let out a slow sigh and said, "I don't know."

Her eyes grew hard as she looked across the table. "The people in the board room at Hollister Publishing think your style is terrific and believe a mystery or thriller or something like that would sell a million copies easily. I mean, they would be open to a historical mystery/thriller if you prefer to keep the trend you've started. But, they want you to give the modern thriller idea serious consideration."

"Give me a couple of days to think about it."

"I'll call you at the end of the week."

I looked at my watch blurting out, "Oh, no. We need to leave now if you're going to make the next flight."

The waiter brought the bill. Holly took it. "This one's on me, again."

"On you?"

Holly chuckled as she said, "Well, at least let me pretend

to be paying for it, okay?"

"What about me pretending to pay you your ten percent?"

Without even a glance, she stood and said, "Let's go."

We walked to the curb where Holly's cab was waiting. She got in and reached out through the window.

"Jay, I'd take Hollister's suggestion very seriously if I were you. Although your novels are selling well, these last two haven't sold anywhere near as many copies as your other six. At this rate, you'll be without a publisher inside of two years."

"I know, Holly. That's why I didn't say 'no.' I'm not an idiot when it comes to business affairs; I just need to make sure that this is the right thing for me at this stage of my career. It'll be a big change."

"I'm with you. Just don't wait too long."

She leaned forward and said to the driver, "Let's go."

The cab drove off toward the airport.

I stood there for several minutes watching the car round the corner, then I walked to Duval Street and turned north toward my apartment.

Along the way I passed several of the regulars strolling or hocking their paintings and other wares and services. I went about two blocks when I came upon old Mr. Jeeter, or at least that's what he said his name was when we met. He was sitting in the same place he always did under the tree in front of what used to be a novelty shop. An old tattered sign in the window read "Going Out of Business Sale Ends Saturday." The building had been empty for several years, even before I arrived.

I stopped and handed him a five-dollar bill just as I did whenever I passed by his spot.

"Thank you, Mr. Morrison. I 'preciates it.

"Don't spend it all in one place."

"I won't."

I wondered for a moment just what must be this old man's story. Could he be the center of a huge mystery that involved beautiful women, cold cash, and maybe even drugs or perhaps a bout with alcoholism?

Probably not, I thought. Just a poor sap down on his luck and stuck at the end of Highway One and no place else to go.

Besides, I thought, nothing exciting ever happens in Key West.

‡   ‡   ‡

ONE WEEK LATER, Holly called. I sat at the window watching the sky as it grew dark and threatening. The rain poured in sheets of abundant water from the sky. Three days of constant rain reflected in my current dilemma. And, I didn't know what I was going to say to her.

People who have lived in Key West for more than a few years seem to think that they deserve the sun shining all the time. They live in paradise where it's supposed to always be sunny with brief respites in the afternoons of a rain storm for about thirty minutes: the typical tropical climate. The sun would reappear and often create an even more hot and humid evening. But, when the sun doesn't shine for more than two days, people often got cranky and feeling that they've been deprived of a valuable commodity. That's my attitude, as well.

"Hi, Holly," I said into the phone without a lot of enthusiasm.

"Jay? What's wrong? Oh, yea; raining, huh?"

I sat there a moment. "Okay. I guess you want an answer?"

"Am I that predictable?"

"No, Holly. You said you'd call me back in a week for my answer. It's a week later – almost to the minute. So, you call."

"What do you think?"

"Okay."

"Okay, what?"

"Okay. I'll do it."

"I knew you would. Now, what are you going to write about?"

"What do you want from me, Holly? I just said I would. I haven't got a clue what I could write about."

Holly chuckled into the phone. "Fine, Jay. When you finish this sunken ship book we'll talk about your next one. Okay?"

I breathed a deep sigh of relief. "That's fine with me. Give me a few months to finish up. Let's say we talk again in September or October. Is that okay with you?"

"No."

"No?" I repeated, puzzled.

I could almost hear the smile in Holly's voice as she said, "Lighten up, Jay. I'm just kidding. Of course it's okay. I was just poking at you. That's all."

I frowned as I looked through the window at the rain as it continued to pour, causing a small flood-like flow through the street.

"I'm not in the mood. I'll talk to you in the fall." With that dismissal I hung up the phone.

"That bitch," I said out loud. "Who the hell does she think she—"

I stopped.

I'm the one in a bad mood, I reminded myself. It ain't her fault. Call her back and apologize. Mother taught me to always make amends for anything I might have said or done that hurt or embarrassed someone else.

I continued looking out the window oblivious to the wind and rain thinking how much I missed my mother's kindness and gentleness of nature. I remembered how she used to cuddle me at the end of a long day when the bullies in school would hound me about my hair. It always seemed so unkept.

No one could help with that little mop that would stick straight up. In fact, one of the reasons I decided to play football was so I could shave my head and no one would notice or even care. For almost twenty years now I had been bald; and I didn't care.

The thought struck me: A murder mystery in Key West?

I picked up a notepad with a lot of numbers scratched on it and a title at the top: "Key West Crime Rates for the Past Twenty Years." I looked it over and thought, No real murders in twenty years to speak of. And the few that did happen were solved in only a few days.

I put my head in my hands and looked out at the rain

falling and the water as it formed a river in the street and thought, what the hell did I just agree to?

THREE

Thursday, June Eleventh

I'M NOT SURE JUST WHY, but after finishing a couple of chapters of my book, I called Brian. The story had finally come together, and I was ready to get it done. I needed to concentrate on the murder mystery before me.

When he answered, I said, "Brian, do you have some time to listen as I run a story idea past you?"

"Of course, Jay. For you? Anything. But, we'll have to get together here at the club. I've got a rehearsal at about one-thirty. Is that okay?"

"Well, the food's not all that good at the outside bar, but okay."

I hung up and finished getting dressed.

I don't know why I liked Brian. He's at least ten years younger than me and a bit immature. And that "on stage" persona just hangs around his neck like a ten-pound necklace with no obvious use or beauty. But, he's creative. And he appreciates my weird ideas.

I arrived a few minutes before Brian, ordered a large cherry cola, then sat at one of the tables near the street. I watched as Brian sauntered along the sidewalk as if he knew people were watching him. He had told me once that he walked that way specifically for that reason. When he said that, I couldn't help myself but try not laughing which caused me to choke out loud. So, I pretended to have caught something in my throat.

Brian is the performer; not me. So my attempt at acting resulted in a knowing smile creeping across my lips.

"You seem to be happy this morning," I spoke through a smile as he walked up to the table. He pulled out a chair, raised his hand, and called out to the bartender, "One Bloody Mary. And go light on the tomato juice."

"Hung over?" I said as my grin widened.

"Shut up, Jay. I'm the one at this table that drinks. So, keep your sarcasm to yourself. And, as a matter of fact, I am happy this morning. Lots have happened. And I'll tell you everything once I've gotten a little more vodka down me and maybe a hamburger, as well."

"I can't wait to hear all about your escapades. I just hope I have some time to ask your opinion on a new idea before you have to be at rehearsal."

"No problem."

Just then, the bar-keep sat a rather weak-looking drink on the table; he sat my cherry cola down as well. I heard a muffled "humph" coming from his lips.

"You got a problem with the order?" I enquired.

"No sir. It's just that..."

"I know. You figure you won't get much of a tip from me since I don't imbibe. Right?"

"I didn't say a word," he mumbled as he walked back to the bar where he pretended to be busy cleaning up.

"You shouldn't give him such a hard time." Brian said as he chuckled aloud. "He's only been working here for about a month. But, he knows that he has to do the day-shift in the outside bar so he can earn the privilege of tending the inside bar where the big bucks flow."

"I know. So, here's my dilemma. My publisher is wanting me to write a murder mystery or a political thriller instead of my normal historical novels."

"Hey, I understand. But, if you write something that more people will buy, they'll make more money, and so will you. I don't see the problem."

I swirled the straw around in the glass in front of me as I thought about what to say next. I think my face was drooping because Brian said, "You'll be okay, Jay. You're a great writer. Besides, you might benefit from a change of genre."

"I'm not a mystery writer, Brian. I'm really good at research. And I'm good at writing about things that happened a long time ago. Besides I'm not too adaptable to change."

Brian's head went back as a bit of Bloody Mary spewed from his mouth.

"No shit, Sherlock! I heard the stories of what you were like when you first moved here. You were a wreck."

"Yeah, I know. But, I'm going to do it."

"Good."

"But, I need a story line. I did the research and discovered that over the past twenty-five years, nothing has happened in Key West that could even pretend to be a murder."

"And your point is what?" Brian stated dripping with pure irony in his voice. "I mean, make up something. Isn't that what fiction writers are supposed to do?"

Actually, I had to smile at that comment. He caught me with my tongue flat on the table. No excuses. I had no recourse.

"Besides, he continued, "something has happened, or should I say something is about to happen that just might make a great story line."

"What?" I said allowing my eagerness to sit in the air for several seconds.

"Oh, I'm not ready to spill that just yet. You'll have to wait until later."

"You're not going to pull that dramatic stall on me, are you?"

"Not really, Jay. I guess I can tell you what I know to this point."

Just then the waiter walked out of the kitchen door near the back of the porch and took our orders for lunch. It was now nearly noon and about twenty other people had gathered for the noon hour meal while we were talking.

"So, here's what I heard through the grapevine. A church in Miami has applied for a permit to have a float in the Fantasy Fest Parade this year."

I laughed out loud and said, "Which church is it?"

"The Christian Center."

"Oh, wow. That's one of the big ones. Their pastor is hot on building his group into a small denomination, I hear."

"So, you think they could pull it off?"

"Oh, yeah. You bet. They've got some big bucks behind them. Several major politicians and business people are members and/or sympathizers with what that guy is doing."

"Well, there's a meeting tonight of the parade committee. They're supposed to be deciding on whether the group gets one of the spots in the parade."

As we were talking, two of the band members arrived and drifted over toward our table.

Harvey, who is the bassist, jumped into the conversation at this point with, "Can anyone attend the meeting when they talk about the application?"

"I don't know," Brian responded. "But, you might want to call Lolita Johansen. I heard she's on the committee,"

Harvey walked out of earshot of the others and pulled out his cell phone. He dialed and spoke quietly. When he returned to the table, Ernie asked, "What did you find out? Is the meeting open to the public?"

"Yeah. Starts at seven at the old city hall building. You want to go together?"

"What time do you want to meet?"

"Why don't we meet at the Blue Parrot for a drink before we go?"

"Sounds good to me," Brian answered.

At this point, the other members of the band arrived and they all went into the main hall and began their practice.

As Brian stood he asked me, "You coming, too?"

"Are you kidding? I wouldn't miss this little circus for anything. Some of the best entertainment we've had here in years." Realizing what I had said, I added, "Uh, present company excluded, of course."

Brian smiled, reached over, gave me a hug, and then ran off into the club.

Four

Later, Thursday, June Eleventh

ODELL, BRIAN, ERNIE, AND HARVEY sat nursing their drinks at the Blue Parrot laughing at Odell's wry sense of humor. As they sat enjoying the moment, Odell stood and walked toward the outdoor bathroom in the back just as I arrived at the table.

Brian grabbed a free chair near the fence and pulled it up for me to sit.

Harvey looked over at Brian and said, "You know, I think we've got the best band in the world."

"Yeah," Brian smiled as his face appeared flushed. "But I think we'd have the greatest band if we added a horn section."

"I'm with you on that," Harvey almost shouted. "I've

thought we could be tight with three guys who could wail something fierce on horns."

He reached over and placed his hand on Brian's leg.

Brian looked down, his eyes squinting a slight shock, he pulled his leg away with a smile and said, "I think I'll talk to Ruthie about it tomorrow. Hopefully, she'll agree."

At that moment, Odell walked up. "I guess we'd better go to the meeting. It's quarter to seven."

We walked down Whitehead to Caroline, then down to the Old City Hall building where the parade committee for Fantasy Fest and about two hundred other people had already gathered. As we entered we could hear people all around us discussing the unusual request from the Christian Center of Miami. Yet, the committee meeting had not begun.

After the new city hall was completed, the Old City Hall of Key West was converted into a building for all city organizations and groups of citizens to use as a meeting hall, concert facility, and dance hall. But the building was most often referred to as the Gay Community Center since almost every event held there in recent years had been sponsored by local gay organizations.

Five months prior to the beginning of Fantasy Fest each year, the various organizing committees would start meeting twice a month to go over the applications for parade participants, floats, and other activities. This year, the man chairing this committee meeting was an old friend of Key West, Perry Savant; a transplant from New York City.

At sixty-two years, he looked a lot older as a result of too many years on the streets of Brooklyn and upper Manhattan first as a beat cop in Queens then as a detective in the major case squad, and finally as deputy commissioner for investigative services, the chief of all the detectives in New York City.

But after twenty-five years on the force, an unexpected scandal arose with people accusing him of misconduct that resulted in his early retirement. So, with a hundred and fifty-thousand-dollar bonus check and a monthly pension that would more than meet his needs, Perry Savant left the NYPD a broken and sad man. He bought a car and drove the fifteen hundred miles from Manhattan to Key West.

Ten years later, Perry found himself in the hospital in Miami undergoing a battery of tests to find out just why he was losing weight, running a constant low-grade fever, and had swollen lymph nodes. After several days of testing, the doctor confirmed the diagnosis that shook Perry to the very core of his being: He was suffering from HIV/AIDS.

The doctor recommended that he start a series of treatments using a new cocktail of drugs the CDC had recently suggested in an effort to hold the disease at bay. Being the fighter that he was, Perry agreed to start as soon as possible.

Now, after fourteen years as a prominent resident of Key West, he was serving as the chair of the parade committee for Fantasy Fest. Honored, yet exhausted from the ravages of his disease, he mustered up as much strength as he could in order to fulfill his obligations.

As he hit the gavel on the table, Perry called the meeting to order. "We need to start this meeting, everyone," he said in a soft voice that no one could hear above the din of conversations. He mustered a little more strength and tried to shout, "Please!"

Sitting next to Perry was one of a toughest looking people you'd ever want to meet named Lolita Johansen; a true native, born and raised in Key West by a family of natives. Since the majority of the residents of Florida are transplants from other states or are snow birds, native status was a matter of pride for those born in the state.

Lolita was often heard declaring that she was a proud citizen of the Conch Republic through and through. She was referring to an incident that occurred on April 23, 1982 after the U. S. Border Patrol set up a blockade on US Highway One just north of the Keys, the single auto route to the mainland. Key West Mayor Dennis Wardlow had appealed to the federal court in Miami to void the blockade to no avail since the order was labeled a national security issue.

The next day, he invited the press to Mallory Square where he read a Declaration of War between the Conch Republic (made up of all the keys) and the United States of America. He turned and surrendered to the Base Commander of the Key West Naval Air Station and demanded one billion dollars in war reparations. Everyone had a good laugh. But as a result of that little charade which made national headlines, the border patrol lifted the blockade with apologies from the State Department.

Lolita stood up and shouted, "Shut up and sit down!"

Being a Florida native was not just a label Lolita wore with pride, she also relished being called a dyke. She would tell people that the idea of being an impenetrable wall fit her personality and attitude well. She could hold her own with just about any man since she was both a weightlifter and an outspoken advocate of the gay lifestyle. She was now Perry's vice chairperson and sometime body guard.

So, when she stood and shouted, the result was a room almost quiet enough for a mouse to feel comfortable enough to come out of hiding. People throughout the room took their seats like scared school children after being caught by the teacher unexpectedly entering the room.

Perry looked up at her and placed a gentle hand on her arm as she sat back down.

"Thank you, Lolita," he said with a vocal smile. He pulled a microphone close to his mouth and turned to the audience.

"I'm sorry that my health is failing. I hope I live long enough to see this celebration."

The audience began to chatter a bit. Everyone knew he was correct, but they wanted to at least make the effort of denying the reality for his sake. Lolita spoke to him in an uncharacteristically gentle voice. "Please don't talk that way, Perry. You know how much we all love you."

"Thank you for your confidence. But, my body tells me otherwise." He picked up a note pad and continued, "Now, for the first agenda item, Salina has a few words for us."

Salina Mathis was an obvious transgender person who was still undergoing the treatments and operations necessary to do a radical sex change. She was about three-quarters of the way to changing from male to female. She already had breast implants, and the laser treatments on her face had removed most of her beard; but she had not had her Adam's apple removed from her throat, and her hips were still narrow.

Salina stood tall and a bit unsure of her footing in a new pair of spiked heels. She looked out at the audience and heard a few sneers and chuckles. A few days earlier, she had undergone plastic surgery on her eyes and nose. The bruising and puffiness in her cheeks and around her eyes declared this recent work. Otherwise, her slim five foot eight body was graceful and beginning to look more and more female.

"Well, ladies, you'll just need to excuse the way I look. The doctor has promised that he'll be finished with everything before the parade. So I'll be taking my place as queen of Fantasy Fest and looking far better than most of you could even wish for."

A lone voice cried out, "In your dreams, bitch!"

Her eyes squinting and a tear rolling down her left cheek, Salina looked to her left and asked, "Who said that? You come up here and say that to my face."

Lolita stood and put her arm around Salina's shoulders and said, "I hope the doctor knows what he's doing, dear. You don't look like the queen of the parade just yet." There was a burst of laughter throughout the hall as Salina pushed Lolita's arm away. "Please darling. At my worst I look better than you."

To that Lolita sat and whispered to Perry, "She wishes."

At this point Perry was done with this little bitch-fest and said, "Please, ladies. We can discuss this further after the meeting is over. We've got a full agenda tonight, so let's return to business, okay?"

Salina relaxed and said, "Of course. Now, before I was so rudely interrupted, I was saying--"

"Bitch. Try to help someone and look what you get." Lolita whispered under her breath.

Salina straightened up and looked over at Lolita. "As I was saying, before I was so viciously bitch-slapped, we have received a record-breaking number of applications for floats for this year's parade."

The crowd applauded.

"But, there is one application we need to deal with. The Christian Center of Miami wants to have a float with the theme 'Every Voice Heard.'"

There was loud shouting and hollering among the group as many expressed their anger at such a request. Salina tried her best to calm down the commotion. "Quiet down, everybody. I feel the same way you do. But, there's a serious issue here. We've argued for years for our right to free, unhindered speech. It seems they are asking for the same thing."

Brian Silver rose to his feet. "Excuse me."

Seeing Brian, Lolita smiled, pointed, and said, "Brian, my darling. Do you have something to say?"

"I understand all this rights business. And of course they have the constitutional right to say what they want and to even preach their opinions. But, don't we have the constitutional right to ask them to say it somewhere else?"

Harvey shouted from where he sat, "Yeah! Right! You tell'em, Brian!"

"Hell! They won't let us come in their churches and tell our side. Why should we let them be in our parade and spout their venom?"

The audience yelled in agreement. Salina smiled. "I

know what you're talking about. I feel the same way."

Brian continued, "Let's vote to reject their application now."

Salina raised her hand to quell the excitement resulting from Brian's call for a vote. As the people calmed down she said, "The mayor told me that since our parade is a public event using public facilities and streets, we may not be able to stop them."

"I could stop them!" Lolita spoke out from her seat at the front.

Salina paused, took a deep breath, and continued, "Anyway! She's looking into it."

"But they don't have to be in our parade, do they?" Ernie shouted.

Salina slowed her pace. "She suggests we wait 'til she receives an opinion from the state attorney's office."

Perry reached up and tapped Salina and said, "That's a good way to put it. We'll keep postponing."

Raising her voice, Salina spoke with authority. "I recommend that we accept all of the applications except the one from Christian Center. That one I move we table until we obtain an opinion from the Mayor's office and our attorneys."

Perry smiled and said, "Okay. We have a motion from the parade committee. All in favor say, 'Aye.'"

Although reluctant to do it, the committee voted "Aye!" Perry pulled out a couple of sheets of paper and held one up and said, "Okay, now that we've got that little bit of business out of the way, for now, let's turn to a couple of other items."

At this announcement the bulk of people in the chamber

filed out of the hall. I made my way down to the front to sit in on the rest of the business. I watched as Salina sat down, turned to Perry, and said, "Looks like they're not all that interested in the rest of the business we have."

"I'm not surprised," Perry replied. "The word spread like wild fire about The Christian Center's application. I think most everyone was afraid we were going to let them into the parade."

"I am so proud of you," Lolita said, "for suggesting at the last meeting that we use this strategy. That was a stroke of genius. All we have to do now is write them and say their application is on temporary hold. We can let them know that when we get an opinion from our legal advisors about the appropriateness of an out of town group participating in a locally sponsored event, we'll let them know."

"That won't hold them for long at all. They'll press it hard with their attorneys."

"You mean this isn't over, Perry?" Salina replied a bit taken aback.

"Heavens, no, darling. We've just begun to fight."

Lolita reached over and touched Perry on the hand. "Perry, I didn't want to say anything in front of the crowd, but are you okay? I don't mean to pry, but you don't look so good."

Perry turned away for a moment then said with a quiet voice, "I've been having night sweats and constant headaches that are almost debilitating. And my strength is failing more than ever."

Salina gasped as Perry continued.

"The doctor is concerned because my white blood cell

count is way too low. So, I'll be taking another trip to Miami next week for more treatments."

"Oh, God, no. I mean I've been going to church every morning and lighting a candle just for you. I've asked God not to let you die."

"Salina, honey, you are so sweet. I appreciate that about you. But I'm only human and I am dying. I hope I survive long enough to be in the parade, but I'm not going to put any money on it."

Just then, Theodore Prejean entered and came up behind Perry, put his hands on his shoulders and said, "I'm sorry, but it's time for Perry's medications. I need to take him home now."

Perry reached up and took Theo's hand. Then with a tear in his eye, he looked up at him, and back at Salina, and said, "I'm the luckiest man in the world to have such a wonderful partner."

Lolita reached over and touched Perry's hand and said, "You go on home. Salina and I will take care of the rest of this business."

Perry nodded and slid back into the wheelchair. Theodore wheeled him out of the room and out the door. The other three members of the committee joined Salina and Lolita around the table and busied themselves with the other items on the committee's agenda.

Outside, the evening was calm. The stars stared down as if they were watching in great concern for this pitiful old man being wheeled home by a handsome, strong, young Louisiana native.

Harvey and I followed them for several minutes as we

made our way back toward the Ta-Da Club.

We all walked for several minutes in silence, passed Sloppy Joes, and turned right on Duval Street.

I quickly caught up with Perry and inquired as to his health. His reply was not what I expected.

"Ah, Jay. Just the man I was thinking about."

"What's up, my friend?"

"I was wondering if it would be okay with you if we stopped by for coffee in the morning at your place."

"Sure. I'll have a pot ready by eight."

"Good. I'll be there at nine."

We both smiled as Theodore wheeled Perry back around headed for home.

"I love these cool evenings," Perry said.

Theodore grunted his approval as they continued walking the half block or so up Duval Street where they turned and walked the one block to Perry's house set back down a small alley known as Charles Street.

As they started down Charles, I could hear Perry say, "Theo, I got a bad feeling about this Christian Center business."

"What is it, Perry?"

"I can't put my finger on it, but I think we'd better secure more information. I think we're in for a fight in this matter; a fight we may not be able to win."

"Why do you say so?"

"Just call it instinct honed on the streets of New York City. I just have a churning deep down in my gut. This parade float thing seems like the beginning of something much bigger."

"Well," Theo continued. "Let's hope you're wrong."

I turned and walked away with an aching inside for eavesdropping on my friends. Yet, I wondered if perhaps Perry wanted to delve into my personal knowledge of Evangelical Christianity hoping to find a jewel of information that might help him in what could be the last major fight of his life.

Five

Friday, June Twelfth

THE NEXT MORNING, I assumed my normal spot in front of the window churning over in my mind the events and conversations that transpired the day before. I knew that my guests would be arriving shortly. I glanced around to assure myself of the apartment's ability to accommodate a wheelchair.

My home was well furnished and appointed with expensive paintings and decorations reflecting my success as a writer. One book shelf next to the desk housed copies of all the books I had written. On the other shelves sat reference works and other novels that I held as literary models, books I believed helped me to learn how to write well.

At the sound of a knock at the door, I took another look and knew Perry would be fine. "The door's open. Come on in."

Perry and Theo entered.

"Perry! How are you?"

"I may be weak but I can still kick your sorry little ass," he said as he stretched out his hand to shake.

After shaking hands I said, "And Theo, how are you?"

"Fine, Jay."

Perry watched Theo as he walked over, sat on the sofa, and picked up a magazine to thumb through. Perry looked over at me and said, "I'm so lucky to have such a wonderful friend who takes care of me. I just love him so much."

"We all love Theo, Perry. He's an angel."

Theo grunted, "Humph."

"So, to what do I owe the honor of a visit from Key West's most famous flamer?"

"Well, I need your advice on something."

"Advice? From me? Uh, sure. Anything you want."

"Well, I could say this nicely, I guess; but that ain't my style, so here it is: You're the only real Christian I know; well, except for Salina. But she cusses a lot and even blows a little weed now and then."

"Salina's got a good heart. And she talks about going to Mass all the time."

"I know."

There was a brief but noticeable pause. Perry continued, "I need to know about this evangelical business. You seem to know a lot about those kinds of things."

"I'm no expert."

"Yes. Well that may be so, but you're the only Evangelical I know. Yet, you don't push that in people's faces, you know?"

"I appreciate you saying that, I think."

"So, I've come to you for advice."

"Boy, what a setup," I said attempting a bit of levity. "But I can't believe I've been so rude. Would you and Theo like a cup of coffee?"

"Sure," Perry said as Theo nodded in agreement.

I walked into the kitchen but could hear Theo as he said, "Perry, darling. Just ask him."

"I know. I will."

A few minutes later, I brought out a tray with three cups of coffee, cream, sugar, and three spoons.

"Please, help yourself."

They each took a cup and fixed it to their liking. I placed the tray and items on a side table and sat at my desk and took several sips of the warm liquid. After a moment I turned toward Perry with an expression that begged for him to begin.

Perry took a couple more sips of coffee and said, "It seems that the largest church in Miami has targeted Key West as their new, uh, what do they call it?"

"Mission field?"

"Yea. Mission field. In fact, they're planning a major event for the same time in October as Fantasy Fest in addition to the application for a float in the parade. That's why we decided to simply put them off for now.

"Okay. You may win this year; but they'll take it to court and win for next year."

Perry sipped on his coffee more and seemed to be thinking through my statement. "I'm afraid this may end our parades as we know them."

"What do the lawyers say?"

"They haven't gotten back to us, yet."

"Well, in a way, that's good. It's not your fault the delay may take too long for them to be approved in time for the parade."

"Yes, but, they're coming anyway. The mayor told me yesterday they applied for a permit to put up a tent and hold meetings on the open field near the Dolphin Research Center--that park area owned by the city at the end of Southard."

"I take it that the mayor doesn't have grounds for refusing their application?"

"That's what she said. Even though the tent will hold about a thousand people, the field is plenty big enough to handle that many cars and more."

I pondered what Perry had said as I took another sip of coffee.

"Sounds like they've done their homework. So what do you want of me?"

"My question is simple. How can we battle this group?"

"Battle?"

"Yes. This is war."

"Like the war on terror?" The words were just off my lips when I realized just how inappropriate that comment was. "Sorry about that. Anyway, I can assure you that they feel they're fighting a spiritual battle against evil. But, referring to it as war? Well--"

"It is," Perry said with a sternness I had not heard from him.

I took a big breath.

"Look, I'm a bit conflicted here. I've learned to appreciate and love this community and all the friends I've made while living here. And you are among my favorite people."

"I know."

"But, I understand both the theological and social positions these people hold. In fact, I hold many of those same beliefs."

Perry seemed visibly shocked by what I said and appeared to ponder it for a moment.

"I guess I never thought of you that way."

"I know," I replied. "You have to understand that I might be theologically opposed to the gay life-style, I do, however, thoroughly appreciate other people's points of view. Everyone has a right to their own opinions. And I always allow other people to be what they are without any judgment on my part.

"I know that, as well."

"But that doesn't mean that I agree with them on everything. In fact, I'm uncomfortable with their approach to evangelism. Sometimes we must simply agree to disagree on things. In my opinion, the key is not to be disagreeable about our disagreements."

"And I appreciate that about you."

"Please understand," I stumbled to continue, "I simply want to be Christ among the people I care about. I'm not here to beat anyone over the head with a twenty-pound bible."

Theodore's eyes widened as he looked up and said, "Do people do that?"

Perry and I both laughed. I said, "It's just a figure of speech, that's all."

"I understand and appreciate that you reflect the Jesus I've heard about all my life," Perry added. "And perhaps you're one of the reasons I'm not openly hostile toward Christianity."

"Wow, Perry, I appreciate that."

"But your friends--"

"Wait a minute," I interjected loudly. "I never called them my friends. I don't know them. I do know you and I consider you my friend."

Perry nodded. "It looks like these folks are ready and willing to swing their bibles at us--" Stopping, he looked over at Theo, smiled, and said, "So to speak."

I grabbed the opportunity and continued, "Perry, please believe me when I say that I might have similar beliefs with these people, but where we might disagree is their methodology. I mean, they may be very sincere in their beliefs and in what they believe God wants them to do. I disagree with their style of 'in-your-face' confrontational religion. I think it's anti-productive. I've gained more through loving kindness than being pushy."

"You do have a rather laid-back way of showing and talking about your personal beliefs. And in a strange way, I sort of admire that. I mean, I can respect their beliefs and their right to have those beliefs. I wish they would do it someplace other than Key West at this particular time."

"I think we both feel the same way about that."

"So, will you help us combat this style of what you call 'in-your-face' method of proselytizing?"

I found myself pausing for a moment because I wasn't sure what to say next. "I'll have to give this some thought."

"Oh?"

"I don't mean I'm not going to help you. I mean I'm not sure just what to do. This is big and complicated."

"I didn't mean to cause problems for you."

"No problem, my friend. Let's just call it a challenge."

"In that case, I'm glad." Perry turned his wheelchair toward Theo. "Let's go."

Theo got up and followed him as he headed toward the door. "Call me as soon as you've come up with something."

"I'd love you guys to stay and have some lunch."

"Thank you, Jay. You're very kind. But, we need to go. I've got a treatment session in Miami this afternoon and we have to hit the road."

"I hope it helps." I paused for a moment then continued quietly, "It breaks my heart seeing you like this."

"It hurts all of us," Theodore replied.

"You may not know this," Perry added before leaving, "but my grandfather was a Baptist preacher. Years ago."

I looked at him with concern. "Did he accept you?"

"He never knew what I am. He died before any of that came out. He was very proud of my being a cop. He passed away a year after I became a detective."

"I'm sorry."

"But, given what I'm facing today, there's something inside me that wants to ask-" Perry paused.

"What?"

Perry rose from his wheelchair as Theodore helped him. He took my hand.

"Perhaps, if you don't mind, could you, maybe, say a prayer for this poor old bastard?"

I stood motionless for several seconds. But I managed a smile. "Of course I will."

"Thank you for everything," Perry said with a tear slowly creeping down his cheek. "You've been a good friend for many years."

I carefully placed my hand on Perry's shoulder and bowed my head. "May God bless and keep you and hopefully heal you."

I leaned closer to him and quietly said, "Be well, my friend. And remember that these things always seem to have a way of working themselves out."

Perry sat back down in the wheelchair with a pained smile. He and Theodore left through the front door and out to the porch where Theo moved the wheelchair down the three steps to the sidewalk.

I walked over to the window and peered out wiping away a couple of tears that creased their way onto my cheek. I watched as Perry and Theodore walked toward Duval Street and turned toward the north. Perry's questions and conversation caused my thoughts to return to the time when I had a serious crisis of faith while attending Emerson College. I had responded to an invitation from another student and started meeting with a group of people who had been raised in the Episcopal Church like I had.

Although I did not consider myself religious, I did find

the camaraderie comforting and familiar. I would attend Sunday morning services at the historic Trinity Church just a few blocks away from the campus. Three months later, these same friends introduced me to a religious movement with which I was unfamiliar.

One of the students invited me to a Bible study meeting in his dorm room where they began speaking in what they referred to as other tongues. I had no clue what these guys were talking about, but I was definitely uncomfortable with their aggressive attitude as they insisted that I try it out. I did not want to be impolite so I stayed after several minutes of their insistence. I finally just stood up and said to them, "Listen, I need to think about this. I mean I've never heard of it, and I'm not sure you guys know what you're talking about."

The others tried to talk me into staying, but one step at a time I politely worked my way out into the hall and back to my own room. There I got down on my knees and tried to do something I had not done over the last ten years. I prayed for help.

"God, help me understand people."

I remained on my knees for several minutes not sure just what I was expecting. Nothing happened. For ten minutes I stayed there with my eyes closed. That's when I heard the door open and my roommate say, "Jay?"

"Uh--"

"What are you looking for?"

"Nothing. I think I was praying."

"You think?"

"Yeah. I know it sounds weird. Sorry."

"Hey. No problem. You do what you've got to do. I'm cool with that."

"Charles, I think what life is all about is finding your own center; not forcing other people into what you think their center should be."

"What?"

I stood up, reached over, stretched out my hand to my roommate, and said, "Thanks."

Charles looked at me and said, "You're welcome?" as we shook hands.

I sat down and pulled out a book I needed to read for a class the next day. I think I had learned a very valuable lesson about people as I wondered, did God just answer my prayer? I sat at my desk, smiled, and went to work on my reading.

With a warm feeling that those memories brought, I returned to reality and went to the computer and the novel that hung around my neck like an albatross. I just had to finish this thing.

About an hour later, I saw Brian walking by the house. I pushed the window open wider and leaned out.

"Brian! You got a minute?"

Brian turned his head, his eyes widening, and said, "Coming." I pushed the window back down, walked over to the door and opened it a little. I walked over to the small kitchen area and poured two cups of fresh coffee as Brian walked in and said, "What's up, Jay?"

"Perry came by to talk to me."

"Perry? Really? Wow. What an honor. He doesn't visit people."

"I know. But that's not why I asked you up here."

"So, I ask again. What's up?"

"Have a seat."

He sat down as I handed him the coffee. I looked at him, my eyes drooping and my face shouting reluctance, and said, "It's about Miami."

"I try to forget that part of my life."

"I know. We've talked about those days several times. But, I need some help with something. It concerns Perry."

"Oh? Well ask away."

"I don't remember you ever mentioning this, but are you familiar with a church known as The Christian Center?"

Brian took a slow deep breath then answered, "Yea. Why?"

"What can you tell me about them?

"Not much."

"I was under the impression that you might have had a relationship of some kind with one or some of the people."

"I do, uh, did." He paused for what seemed nearly a minute.

I couldn't tell whether his expression was signaling fear or just hesitation. "Well, what can you tell me?"

"I'd rather not talk about it." Brian got up and walked over to the bookshelf where I kept all the books with my name on the spine, each with its own title. He ran his fingers over several of them and said, "I wish I could write. I'd love for people to read my stuff after I'm dead."

"Not much money in it. You make a hell of a lot more than I do with your singing."

"The thought of someone reading what I had written

long after I'm gone; well, that's cool. Kinda makes you feel, you know, sort of immortal."

"Why has this pastor made Key West his latest mission field?"

"Do you really want to know?"

"No. Perry does."

"I can't say for sure. You'll need to talk to Maria, a friend of mine. She's on the Missions Committee, I think. But, I'm not surprised they're targeting Key West."

"Do you know the pastor? I think his name is Santos."

"Actually, his name is Juan Diego Hernandez y Santos. At least that's what his name was when he emigrated from Cuba."

"I've seen him on television. I didn't realize he was Cuban."

"I think he may have been forced to leave Cuba. But I don't really know for sure. Just rumors, you know."

"Wow," I verbalized aloud.

"I think he came over with a friend of his or they may have met up after they both got here. I'm not sure what his real name is but he calls himself Marcus Champion."

"I think that's the man who is coming to Key West in a few weeks to set up things for a tent revival. At least that's the scuttlebutt."

"If he's coming here, then Pastor John will be down soon. Marcus is the front man and John is the celebrity."

"Sounds like a racket."

"I think they were both some kind of con men in Cuba when they were young."

"They must have had a conversion."

"I don't think so," Brian said quickly. "They just found a more legal way of conning people out of their money."

"Whoa, man. That's cold."

"Trust me. They aren't any different now than they were in Cuba. At least that's what I've heard."

"They could give Christians a bad name, if that's true."

"I know you have a Christian background."

"Yeah."

"Well, I'd listen to you talk about God any day. But, those men? They have nothing to say to me or anyone else as far as I'm concerned."

"Can you give me a little background?"

"Is this about what happened last night?"

"Yes. Perry came to me about it."

"Okay, let me give you a little background. The church is located in a section of southwest Miami where local residents complained for years. You know, the traffic was awful every day of the week. Hundreds of cars coming and going all day, every day."

"I can't imagine."

"And, of course, on Sundays, thousands of cars parking everywhere; in the lots, the green areas of the church property, and any available spaces for blocks in every direction. I guess that Pastor Santos hadn't planned on that kind of growth."

"I'll bet that caused quite a controversy."

"What set off a firestorm of protest was the announcement that the church was planning to build a five story parking garage in the middle of that residential area. The local neighborhood association approached the church leaders several times about the problem."

"So what happened?"

"Well, it seems the church made some very generous offers to the owners of five houses that adjoined the church's property, offers that were quickly accepted. During the next several months those houses were demolished and parking was expanded by another 250 parking spaces on the property."

"Those were expensive parking places."

"It relieved most of the pressure in the community. And it was this type of cooperative attitude that's kept the church free of controversy – until now."

"So why all the hub-bub now?"

Honestly? I have no clue what's going on. And I know nothing about Santos and his side-kick other than what I've already mentioned."

After a moment of reflection, I looked at Brian eye-to-eye.

"What can we do about this parade float thing?"

"Nothing."

"Nothing?"

"Nothing."

"There ought to be something we can do."

"Perhaps something will be done. But, it won't be you."

"Oh?"

"Let's just say that someone will look into the matter and let you know. Okay? Trust me." Brian looked at his watch. "Uh oh, I'm rehearsing my new number with the band in a few minutes. Got to run."

"Are you doing a new number tonight?"

"No. Saturday night. You'll be there?"

"I wouldn't miss it."

"Terrific. See you." Brian shook my hand then quickly moved out the door.

I couldn't help but laugh as I walked over to the window to watch Brian make his way down the street and turn onto Duval.

I walked back to the kitchen, poured myself another cup of coffee, walked back to the window, and pondered what had just happened.

What did Brian mean by saying 'Trust me'? What could Brian be up to? The thoughts swirled around in my head. Whatever Brian was planning, well, it just couldn't be anything good. My thoughts went wild with speculation. Was Brian capable of harming Reverend Santos? And if he was, why would he? What was it about this pastor that would cause Brian to make such a brash statement? And what is it that would cause so much emotional turmoil with people of Key West?

I put my cup down on the windowsill, walked to the door, and left the apartment. The thoughts whirled in my head. I realized that I had to do a lot more investigating to find out just what it was about these two men from Miami that concerned Brian so much.

I stopped walking and stood at the corner. My heart seemed to beat heavy in my chest. I knew what I had to do. But my deepest concern was whether I could find out in time?

S i x

June Thirtieth

PERRY, THEO, AND I finished lunch on Perry's patio as a calming breeze flowed through the trees and cooled the air. Theo picked up the dishes and went into the kitchen leaving me and Perry alone.

Perry leaned back in his lounge chair with a stretch attempting to hide the pain that creased his face. I just knew that if he lived another year he would be lucky. But, I was not going to be the one to spread rumor or spoil the limelight that he so deserved as the parade's Grand Marshal. If he was up to it, he would be leading the parade on Halloween night.

As I sat looking at what was once a dominating figure within the greatest police force in the world; well, let's just say AIDS is a horrible mistress.

A New York City native, Perry applied to the police academy after graduating near the top of his class in high school. He turned down a scholarship to attend Columbia University in order to become one of New York's finest. He knew that if he wanted to continue his education, he could do so at night with the department's blessing.

His natural insight, plus his strength and agility, made him a perfect candidate to be a NYPD police officer. At nineteen he was one of the youngest men to go through the academy. Yet, he was never intimidated nor did he ever shrink from any problem he encountered. He graduated from the academy at the top of his class.

After joining the precinct near his home, Perry proved to be an excellent beat cop and rose to the ranks of detective and was later promoted to Chief of detectives in the Manhattan district by the time he was thirty-five. Bright, intelligent and dedicated to his work he caught the eye of many politicians in New York, some of whom suggested that he should be on the fast track to become Chief of Police and even Police Commissioner one day.

However, all that changed when the people of the city read about a two-bit criminal who accused Savant of misconduct and criminal activity. And now fifteen later, Perry was facing an even more horrible fight: this time for his life.

Sitting before him now, I was determined not to show the pity I felt inside for this man who had become such a good friend. So, I pulled out a notebook I always carried with me to take notes. It was not yet filled with copious notes on this group of people set to invade our little community.

"Okay, Perry. It seems that the Reverend and his assistant were not happy with your letter. Brian talked to some of his contacts in Miami."

"I can't wait to hear this."

"I know. So, it seems that you caught them off guard by not refusing their application. Champion was totally miffed by your explanation of some minor errors and problems with the application itself."

"That was my idea!" Theo yelled through the pass-through window between the patio and the kitchen.

"Get back to your chores, Sweetheart!" Perry leaned forward and spoke in a softer voice. "Actually, Theo did make that suggestion. The attorneys loved it."

"So your explanation of having to wait until the attorneys ruled on what to do must have been brilliant because these guys were incredulous."

"I hoped as much. The attorneys insisted that I use the phrase 'under review.'"

"You know they'll be filing another application next year that will be letter perfect--no mistakes."

"I know. I'm just afraid that they've actually chipped away at our celebration of the gay life-style. I hope they haven't ended it or force it to be changed into something else."

"I was hoping you wouldn't say that."

"Over the next several months, I fully expect these people to prepare for a major religious assault on the beautiful freedom we've enjoyed for so long in our little haven in the sun."

"Yep. And you can fully expect these people to arrive here well before the festival fully armed with every spiritual weapon in their arsenal."

"I know."

"During the last two weeks, I've researched this church and discovered that the coffers are overflowing with cash. Marcus Champion seems to be a financial genius. I mean instead of putting their money into checking and savings accounts where it could easily be traced and accounted for, he's purchased hundreds of expensive paintings and other art works."

"Damn clever!"

"I visualize this man being able walk down the halls of the church quoting the exact price of each painting hanging there. And I'm willing to bet that most people in that church have no clue the value of those innocuous pieces of art that decorate their hallways. I have to admire the hutzpah of this man that Santos claims as a personal friend, confidant and financial advisor."

"I understand. But have you discovered any specifics?"

I handed Perry a couple of sheets of paper. "One of these newspaper articles recounts how Santos and Champion started with a small congregation of about fifty people meeting in Santos's back yard. And now, less than twenty years later, it's a mega-church of over twenty-five thousand people with assets exceeding a hundred million dollars.

Unfortunately, that's where the trail ends. I could find no mention of Marcus Champion or John Santos prior to twenty years ago. I mean, there's simply nothing there. Of course, I took Brian's word that the two men had emigrated from Cuba around the same time. And yet, I just can't dismiss my gut. You know, the facts just don't seem to fit."

"What else is in that mystery-magical notebook you carry around with you?"

I smiled. "It seems that Champion will be arriving in the city by the middle of October. He's supposed to get a large tent erected and ready for Santos' arrival. I don't know that date. They plan to begin a series of evangelistic meetings three or four days before Halloween."

"Okay. So, we've got our work cut out for us. You keep me updated on everything you find out. Oh, and I like the idea of you being an intermediary between me and Brian. I love him to death, but he's way too high maintenance for me to deal with. I'm sure he's a wealth of information. So, encourage him to continue feeding you everything he hears."

"He's promised to keep me informed. Also, I'll continue my research into this church and its leadership. Wait a minute. There was one other thing."

I thumbed through the pages. "Here it is. It seems several highly influential people are members of his church. There's at least two state legislators and one state senator; oh, and one congressman. He has five of the city's richest businessmen on his board of trustees. We're talking heavy hitters. I can only assume that if we get into a court room tussle with these guys they could cause all sorts of problems for us and the city."

"I understand. And thank you for the good work. All I know is that I made a good choice in asking you for advice in this matter."

"We're on the same team. I want to keep this place peaceful, too." And with that I shook Perry's hand, yelled a good-bye to Theo, and slipped out through the patio door.

Seven

October Twenty-ninth

FANTASY FEST BEGAN unofficially with a series of parties and celebrity events the week-end before. The actual Festival started on October twenty-eight with a Wednesday night reception at the Civic Center. A local band from the Elevator Club played as nearly five hundred people crowded into the hall to enjoy the fun and frolicking for which the festival was famous.

I was there, of course, sitting at a table alone as I took notes for the article I had planned to write about this amazing party. A few of my friends came over to greet me and encourage me to "enjoy myself." I told them that writing was my greatest joy.

But, something ached inside me as I watched so many people enjoying each other's company. People all around me were with someone they loved. And although I had not spent too much time thinking about it, I realized that I was totally alone. My parents were both dead and I had no siblings. Worst of all, I didn't even have any cousins with whom I had any kind of relationship. No family at all.

One very attractive young man came over and sat down at my table. He smiled then puckered his lips blowing me a kiss. I smiled back. He reached over to my hand and placed his on top of mine and started to rub it.

Suddenly, a hand reached over and grabbed the young man's hand and pulled it back. I looked up into the eyes of Fatima Sax, Key West's new police chief. She had been hired to lead the city's police department about two months earlier. She looked hard at the young man sitting next to me.

"Hands off, young fella. This man is not gay. And he's a friend of mine. So, I'd appreciate it if you respect his preferences and find someone else to hit on."

The gentleman seemed embarrassed, but apologized and moved on.

I looked up at her and said, "I don't know whether to thank you or slap you for interfering. But, I do appreciate your looking after me."

"Oh, I'm not looking after you, I didn't want you to get started on something at the same time that I wanted to talk to you."

"Okay, chief, what can I do for you?"

"I wanted to ask a favor," she said as she sat in the chair vacated by the other person. "I would like for you to consider writing a tribute to Perry Savant."

"Oh, wow. That would be my honor. So, what is the occasion?"

"I understand that Perry's birthday is coming up the end of next month. And it appears that he is too ill to enjoy these festivities this week. I thought I'd arrange for a couple of dozen of his closest friends to meet together and surprise him with a party."

"He doesn't like big parties; you know?"

"Oh, I know that. But this will be small group. And we'll make it as pleasant for him as possible. Like, we'll keep it low-keyed and no loud noises."

"So, what's my writing a tribute got to do with that?"

"Well, I've arranged for the newspaper to print your piece on his birthday. They're going to make a special edition just for him. And I thought you could do a biography and tribute all in one. It will be the center-piece for the edition. It could be a real feather in your cap, so to speak."

"For Perry and for you? I'd be more than happy to do it. When do I need to get it to the editor at the paper?"

"Well, his birthday is on a Friday, so see that you get it there no later than Tuesday. It's only a weekly, so no big hurry."

I agreed to do it and stood when she did to leave. As I watched her walk away, I felt good inside because I knew that this would make Perry very happy. But, I knew he'd probably make a big fuss over it all.

I sat back down and called for another drink as I continued to write in my book. Probably ten minutes passed by as I wrote when I was interrupted by Theo's voice.

"Hi, Jay. May I join you?"

"Of course, Theo. Your company is a pleasant surprise."

He sat, ordered a drink from the waitress, turned to me, and said, "You know he ran me out of the house, don't you?"

"I figured, as soon as I heard your voice."

"I may be his lover, but I can't do a thing with him. He's always so dictatorial about things. He fussed all evening until I finally just walked out of the house. I know I must have looked and sounded mad, but I don't care."

"Wow. I was just talking about him with Fatima a few minutes ago. Funny that you show up right after that."

"It is. Was she asking you about the big birthday party?"

"Oh, you know about that?"

"Of course. They could never pull that off without me running interference for them. I mean he is a famous detective and can easily put together pieces of evidence. So, anyway, did you agree to our little thing for the newspaper?"

"You know I did."

"Good. I was hoping that you would."

"So, what about tonight?"

"What do you mean?"

"I mean, why don't I go with you and get Perry off that recliner and bring him out to the party."

"Oh, I don't think that's such a good idea."

"Why?"

"Well, I uh, you see —"

"You're scared."

"No I'm not. I mean, well, I guess —"

"How about I go over there alone and get him out?"

"You know, Jay, normally I think I would agree. But, maybe I should tell you that I had to take him to the doctor's office in Miami today. We only got back about three hours ago. I truly think he's just exhausted. And if you go over there, you may wake him up from the sleep he needs so badly."

"Ah, I understand. So, we won't do that."

"Thank you."

At that we both sat back; me leaning my chair against the wall and he sitting up straight with perfect posture like he always did wherever he was.

I watched as Brian Silver walked out onto the stage at the strains of the band playing the opening bars of "People." He began singing Barbara Streisand's signature number — sounding just like the famous singer.

The audience was enwrapped in the beauty of Brian's amazing voice that duplicated the Streisand sound so clearly. At the end I found that I was dabbing away a couple of tears. I also noticed that Theo was crying into his handkerchief like a baby.

"That was amazing," I said sort of to no one.

"I just can't handle that very well, can I?" Theo added.

"Theo, you're just a human. You have emotions."

"I know. I just wish I didn't cry nearly every time that Brian sings. He just does that to me."

Just then we heard a ruckus from the area near the stage. We both jumped up from our seats.

"What's going on," Theo asked.

"I'm not sure," I answered. "Let's see if we can help."

We made our way over to where Brian was in a tussle with another man. Brian's costume and face was a mess as the two wrestled around on the floor. Suddenly, Harvey, one of the band members, jumped into the fray and pulled the guy off of Brian. As he did, Harvey hit the man hard against the side of his head laying the man out cold on the floor.

He helped Brian up and wrapped his arms around him in a big hug. I looked at the young man on the floor but did not recognize him. I looked at Brian and Harvey at the moment when Brian pushed him away from him. He straightened up his wig and walked off in what one might describe as a "huff."

Almost simultaneously, Fatima pushed me aside and lifted the man on the floor to his feet.

"We don't put up with brawls in this town, sir. I'm afraid you'll have to come with me."

I watched puzzled as the man walked sheepishly ahead of the police chief who pushed him toward the door. I turned to Theo and said, "Wow. I wonder if she saw everything and knew exactly who was at fault."

"I don't know anything about that. But, I do know that in this town the one person you do not mess with is Brian. Even if Brian started it, Fatima would arrest the other man anyway."

I watched as Fatima and her prisoner walked out through the back entrance to the hall. I turned to see Harvey walking in the direction that Brian had gone.

"I hope Brian and Harvey are both alright."

"They will be. Those guys in the band look after each other. And they are very protective of Brian. I mean, he's their meal ticket.

I thought about that for a few minutes. I excused myself and left the party. I found it odd that before I was out the door, the party was already rocking harder than it did before Brian's performance. I couldn't help but wonder about this young man who had made such an impression on the residents of Key West.

Eight

THE COMMITTEE PLANNED the climactic parade to begin at 8:00 pm Halloween evening. But by lunch-time the festivities were well underway with small impromptu parades as numerous gay men and women marched in their fanciest costumes. The police kept a close eye on these side shows to prevent any traffic problems, but did not stop them from enjoying themselves.

At a party the night before attended by dignitaries, Brian served as the "mistress" of ceremonies dressed as Barbara Streisand. Those who were attending included the planning committee members and about four hundred people who had paid a hundred and fifty-dollars a plate to attend. The entertainment was a special show developed by Brian and the band with a special appearance by Jennifer Lopez, as performed by Brian Silver, singing her hit song "Everybody's Girl."

The crowd went wild and the ovation lasted almost five minutes with Brian in tears. Ruthie could not have been more proud.

Across town the tent revival had averaged about five hundred people per night with lots of excitement among the Evangelical community. No further protests occurred, and most everyone was busy enjoying the fruits of their labors. The gays celebrated with Fantasy Fest and the Christians enjoyed their revival.

So, Halloween began as any other day that Saturday as Brian walked into the Ta-Da Club at about twelve-thirty in the afternoon. I was helping Ruthie with her accounting, not that I know that much. I think she just needed an extra pair of eyes and some company to help pass the time until the evening's festivities.

When Ruthie saw him approaching, she yelled out the open door of her office, "Brian, get your ass in here. The boys have been waiting on you nearly half an hour to start rehearsal."

He walked over to the door and stuck his head into her office and said, "Sorry, Miss Ruthie. It won't happen again."

"I know, honey, but tonight's important. You're premiering your new number for the general public after the Parade."

"I know."

"So get in there and practice. I want that number to be something people will be talking about for years."

Just then he noticed me sitting there. So he smiled and nodded his head toward me. I indicated a small hello. He continued down the hall and into the main auditorium where the band had gathered on stage. It was odd, but Brian left the door standing open.

Harvey started with, "Well, good of you to join us, Miss Thing!"

"Jealous 'cause your thing ain't as good as my thing?"

"Harvey, leave him be. Let's get to work," Ernie piped in.

"Let's start with the first two." Karl added, "That'll be "Everybody's Girl" on four. Ready? One, two, three, four."

The band played the intro and Brian walked onto the stage acting like Jennifer Lopez. He started singing, but as he got to the words "Act like I'm interested in some other man," Harvey broke out in laughter and nearly fell off the drum stool. The others stopped playing and stared at him. They began to laugh along with him; except for Brian who stared at Harvey with looks that could kill.

Brian paused for a moment.

"Okay, Harvey. What the hell's so funny?"

"I don't know. I guess the words you were singing just got to me. I'm sorry."

Brian shook his head and continued, "Harvey, I've just about had it with your sarcastic looks and phrases. I'm just tired of your antics."

"Me? My antics? You're the prima donna! You're the only one who's right about everything. And I'm tired of it. You hear me? I'm tired of it."

At that, Harvey headed out of the auditorium throwing

his drum sticks high in the air. One hit Ernie square on the head.

"Ow! Harvey!" Ernie yelled as he put his hand on his head and drew it back with a palm full of blood.

"I'm bleeding! Harvey! Harvey!! Come back here, damn it!"

Harvey didn't look back but kept walking toward the door. "Don't you dare come back! You hear me? Don't you ever come back here again! Do you hear me, man?"

At that Ernie walked out of the room as Nelson and Odell put their guitars on their stands and sat on the edge of the stage.

"What's going on in there," I asked Ruthie.

"Dem boys fight all the time. Pay'em no mind."

I leaned out the door and looked into the auditorium where I saw Karl sitting on his stool with his head bowed shaking it back and forth. He spoke up.

"Look, guys, we're all tired. Maybe we should just go get a couple of drinks and rest for several hours before we have to be back for the show tonight."

Ruthie finally got up and walked in as her face seemed to glow brighter and brighter the angrier she got. She had a way of being very calm at first but building to a crescendo. So I assume the guys were as startled as I was when she started in on them as soon as she hit the doorway.

"What the hell's goin' on in here? Harvey just went storming out of the club muttering something about you guys being totally insane."

Karl looked up. "Sorry, Miss Ruthie. We just had a small disagreement. We'll have it together tonight. You know you can count on us."

Ruthie looked over at Brian as the anger flowed effortless from her face. "You okay, honey?"

Brian was sitting on the stage cross-legged at this point. He looked up at Ruthie and said, "I'm okay; just tired."

Ruthie took a deep breath and shook her head as if wondering just what was wrong with these guys.

"I guess the pressure of the festival starting this week, opening a new show, and being expected to be at all the parties that are going on tonight and all."

She stood there appearing to wait for a response that never came. She turned on her heels and walked toward the door. She stopped and shook her head. I could just visualize an internal dialogue going something like: Those guys! Maybe someday they'll grow up. At least that's what I would have been thinking.

She turned back around, looking toward the stage area. She said out loud as if to no one in particular, "I don't think so. Those boys will never grow up." I had to blink twice.

She walked out of the auditorium and back to the desk across from me where she went back hard at work as usual.

That's when I got up and walked to the door just in time to hear Brian say, "We got this stuff down. Once the audience gets here, we'll be itching to get it on. You know, we always gets it done."

Ernie walked back into the room holding a hand full of tissue against his scalp. He sat down next to Karl and said, "I don't know what got into him. I know he's high strung anyway, but, man! This was way out of line."

Karl leaned over and looked at Ernie's head. He pulled

strands of hair back with care as he took the tissue away from the wound. A large gash on top of a blue lump greeted his gazing eye. The blood had not clotted, so he took Ernie by the arm and said, "Get up. We need to go to the hospital and have this thing looked at."

"I'll be fine," Ernie protested.

"Let's just make sure, okay? Besides, one thing's for sure, you're going to have one hell of a headache before the show tonight."

"No kidding."

"Don't forget we need to be back here by ten tonight for the show at eleven. Don't be late," Brian reminded them.

"We won't. See you then."

Ernie and Karl walked past me without saying a word and went out of the concert hall followed by Odell and Nelson who both nodded at me as they left. Brian sat alone in the middle of the stage. He looked up for a long moment staring at the ceiling and the catwalks that crisscrossed the beams where numerous lights glared down on him like so many eyeballs. I wondered what he must be thinking. He shook his head, got up, and walked out of the building.

‡ ‡ ‡

ABOUT 6:00 THAT EVENING the crowds gathered, as always, at Mallory Square to watch the sun go down. They also anticipated the finale of Fantasy Fest: the grand parade of all parades. But tonight more people than normal gathered for sunset. There was great rejoicing and shouting as the people counted down the seconds and the sun sank into the sea. As it disappeared, the digital watch on my arm blinked 6:39 pm.

Just then, Brian entered Sloppy Joes and walked over to the table where I was seated eating a hamburger while I waited for the big parade to start. He stood there for a moment until I looked up with a little shock in my eyes.

He said, "Jay, do you have a moment?"

"For you, anytime, my friend."

He sat.

"I thought you might be able to help me out with a dilemma I'm facing."

"Worried about your show tonight?"

"No. The revival meeting started last night. And, well, I thought I ought to go over there and see what's going on. I mean, I am a member of the church."

"Do you feel a part of that group?"

"Actually, this may sound a bit weird, but I do feel a connection. Those people helped me a lot years ago. I might not be where I am today if it hadn't been for Pastor Santos."

"Wow. I wasn't aware."

"I don't talk about it much. But, I was wondering: should I go or not?"

I sat stunned by the question. I smiled, but had no idea what to say.

"I didn't mean to throw a curve ball."

"Yeah, well, I didn't expect that. But, you know, if you really want to go, I'd be happy to go with you. That might make it easier for you."

"You'd do that for me?"

"Of course, Brian. I count you among my friends around here."

I hailed the waitress and paid my tab. We left the bar and pushed through the heavy crowds on Duval Street and headed toward the park area to the west.

‡   ‡   ‡

WHEN WE ARRIVED, the parking lot was filling fast and we could hear the music coming from the tent.

Although it wasn't yet 6:30, the service had begun with the familiar sounds of "Onward Christian Soldiers" coming from inside the tent. We could hear the strains of a professional sounding orchestra providing the accompaniment to the congregational singing.

Several minutes passed by as Brian stood looking at the tent in the darkness. I encouraged him to walk with me across the street toward the entrance. As we got about halfway through the parking lot, a hand reached out and stopped Brian. He turned, startled.

"Harvey? What are you doing here?"

"That's exactly what I was going to ask you?"

"That's none of your business."

"Anything you do that might jeopardize the future of the band or the club is my business."

Brian looked at him with the curiosity of a small child studying the movements of an ant on the ground.

He sighed and said, "Harvey, you're one that – oh, never mind." He stopped and looked over at me, and said, "I used to attend the church in Miami that's sponsoring this tent meeting. I know these people. I was feeling a little nostalgic and wanted to look in to see what was going on. Curiosity, nostalgia, that's all."

Harvey's face softened as he looked back at Brian then at me. "I was just worried about you," he said as he reached over and took Brian's hand in his, "And I wanted to apologize for saying the things I did at rehearsal. I'm sorry about all that."

Brian allowed a slight smile to crease his face as he withdrew his hand from Harvey's.

"Harvey, you are such a paradox. One minute you seem insane and another you are so precious," but Brian's smile turned sour as he became as serious as a corpse. "But I'm afraid it's going to take a lot more than just saying 'I'm sorry,' you know, to make things right. I mean this isn't the first time you've done or said stupid things."

Brian paused and waited for a reply. Harvey said nothing.

"Oh, come on, Harvey! We work together. You're a terrific drummer! Actually, I think you're the best ever. And I love having you behind me making me look and sound good on stage. Don't you understand? I mean, you cut Ernie's head open and never said a word of apology to him about it. You need to get over to his apartment and let him know you're sorry about causing that gash in his head."

"He didn't go to the hospital?"

"Yes he did. But the cut wasn't as deep as we thought. So the doctor just applied some antibiotics, dressed the wound, and sent him to his apartment. He told him to put a cold press on it until later tonight."

"He's going to be able to play, isn't he?"

"I don't know, Harvey. Damn it. Why do you have to do things like that?"

"I don't know."

"Look, I think you should go and check on him. That's all. He'll appreciate it."

Harvey's countenance turned downcast as he stared back at Brian. Without a sound he turned to walk away.

"Wait, Harvey,"

Harvey stopped as Brian continued.

"Look, I'm sorry that we're not connecting like we used to when we first started, you know? Neither of us is at fault. Really. Let's just shake and be professional about this, okay?"

Harvey turned back and looked at him with a hard stare. He started to say something, looked over at me, and then walked away leaving us standing about thirty feet from the front entrance to the tent.

As if a light turned on, Harvey stopped, turned, and said, "Okay. Why don't we get together later? We can talk then. That'll give me time to calm down and think about things."

"Where do you want to meet?"

"I'll call you."

Brian watched as Harvey strolled to his scooter and left the parking lot. He shrugged his shoulders and turned to me and said, "You ready?"

I nodded and we walked to the door of the tent and looked in. We stood there for several minutes until an usher walked over indicating if he could show us to a seat. Brian shook his head and the man walked away.

Reverend Santos was in the pulpit speaking hard against sin and debauchery. The crowd had responded well over the past two nights, the crowd growing larger with each evening despite the news reports that dominated the local radio and television stations. Tonight the tent was about ninety percent full. Reverend Santos could see Brian standing at the back even with nine hundred people in the audience. He had started his sermon about five minutes earlier. So without skipping a beat, he continued to speak to the crowd.

"Our way of life in these United States is under assault and we are here on the frontline of that battle. Here in Key West sin and debauchery has formed a beach-head and is planning to move into the heartland of our country to infect this great nation with the filthy lifestyle of the people who are grotesquely labelled as 'gay.' They are insisting that we must accept them and let them live the way they want to.

"They insist that there should never be any laws that restrict them from doing whatever they want. But that's exactly what laws are for! We are to restrict people's actions so that the whole community is not contaminated. We've come here to Key West to stop the contamination with the antibiotic of the Gospel of Jesus Christ."

At that, the crowd burst into cheers. Some people leaped to their feet and applauded with great enthusiasm. As the sound died down and the crowd settled, Santos reached over and grabbed a large bible, held it up high, and declared, "Let the deviants of Key West know that we are here to strike a fatal blow to their infection on our society with the Word of God. If you're ready to take a stand for

God, stand to your feet, and say so!"

With those words still ringing in their ears, the members of the congregation stood to their feet and started shouting, "Praise God" and "Homos repent!"

Brian bowed his head, turned, and walked away from the tent as a tear rolled down his cheek. I think that it was at that moment he knew that there was no way that he would ever be able to go home. It must have been like the sharp knife of separation sliced through his heart and severed his connection to the people of The Christian Center of Miami.

‡ ‡ ‡

TEN BLOCKS AWAY from the tent, the big parade of the week-long celebration of Fantasy Fest was underway as a huge crowd formed shouting in loud voices along Duval Street. An impromptu parade of people who were either almost undressed or naked began marching along with the official parade. Many revelers dressed in costumes of various kinds; others were dressed up in their finest, and still others, barely dressed at all.

They all were drinking and partying with tremendous gusto. Since the sun set an hour earlier, the thousands of people on and near the Mallory Square pier joined the festivities on Duval.

When we got back to Sloppy Joes, I went inside as Brian walked off to talk to some of his fans in the crowd. I went in and sat down at the table the waitress had held for me.

At 7:30 PM, Brian stood next to a light pole just behind Sloppy Joes. He had changed clothes and was dressed in one of his finest suits with his signature red scarf wrapped around his neck. He looked handsome enough to have taken from out of a magazine spread. Anyone could see that this was not a vagrant or even a celebrant. But, I saw that he had a serious look of concern on his face as he peered through the crowd.

I sat in Sloppy Joes at a table with a couple of other people when I spotted Brian standing by the light pole. I couldn't help myself but to worry for my friend. Seeing him standing there alone reminded me of two friends from high school that had been drinking too much while celebrating at the prom. The last time I saw them, they were standing under the light pole outside the dance hall making out and holding a bottle of some cheap whiskey.

Of course it wasn't legal for any of us at the prom to be drinking, but who was paying attention? When David Milligan and Lillian Watts left the party feeling good, no one noticed or even cared that David had difficulty with the car keys. And no one seemed to care as they drove off, weaving all over the road.

I'll never forget the morose atmosphere that hung over the school following the accident that took both of their lives. That horrible atmosphere surrounded every one until the school closed for the summer. Those two were some of the most popular kids in high school, and their deaths sent chills throughout the city school system.

The funeral had to be held at the school's football stadium because the family believed that about two thousand people would attend the service. Actually more than five thousand showed up. It was at that occasion that I swore never to drink anything alcoholic as long as I lived. Oh, I slipped a few times when I would drink a beer or two, but I never drank enough to get drunk.

I walked out of Sloppy Joes to see how my friend was doing. The crowd was increasing at a fast pace. I tried to see whether Brian was still at the pole. I was able to make out his signature red scarf and worked my way over to where he was standing.

"Hey, Brian, are you doing okay?"

"Not now, Jay."

"Excuse me," I replied. "Sorry I disturbed your moodiness."

"That's not what I meant. I've just got a lot on my mind right now. I need to think."

"Is there anything I can do?"

"No."

"I'm not trying to pry, but you don't look so good. What's wrong?"

"Nothing. I mean I appreciate you going with me to the tent revival. That was a huge revelation for me."

"So, are you going to be okay for the show tonight?"

"No. Yes. No. No problem. Really, everything is fine."

Brian seemed confused and even more distracted than he was when we had first met and gone to the meeting.

He pulled himself together and said, "I'll be fine. Really. Just be in your seat at the club by eleven and you'll see a show like you've never seen before."

I was disturbed by Brian's actions and attitude, but I knew that if Brian didn't want my help, I couldn't force him to accept it. So, I reached over and placed my hand on

Brian's shoulder and said, "Let me help you, Brian."

Brian brushed my hand away with a gentle swipe and said, "You can't. It's something I have to work out for myself."

"I think friends are supposed to help friends."

"Jay," Brian said, "You really are a good friend. And you've been good to me, especially when I first got here and was so confused about my faith and my sexuality. I'll always cherish your friendship and insights. But, sometimes a person has to do some things alone. I'll talk to you about it tomorrow afternoon. Let's meet for lunch, okay?"

"Okay, Brian. But, if I can help in any way possible before then, you will call me?"

"I'll do that. But look, I need to be alone for a while right now. Do you mind?"

"I only wanted to make sure you'll be okay."

"I will. Don't worry."

I paused for a moment and looked deep into Brian's eyes, smiled, crossed the street, and headed toward Mallory Square in order to avoid the crowds pressing Duval. That's when Theodore stopped me with a friendly, "Jay! What a coincidence."

"Theodore? Good to see you. Where's Perry?"

"He insisted I come out and leave him at home. I didn't like that at all. I really feel bad out here. I mean, I'd rather be sitting at home with him, you know?"

"I understand how you feel."

"He's in pain and doesn't want me to watch."

"He also wants you to go out and have some fun. You're young. He wants you to enjoy your youth."

"That's nice of you to think that about Perry. He is special, Theo said a little embarrassed."

"Still, that's not the way to treat someone who cares for you, is it?"

Animated, Theo said. "I didn't think so either. How can I have fun knowing he's back there all by himself and in pain?"

"Come with me."

"Where're we going?"

"We're going over there and get that man out and into the fresh night air so he can enjoy the fun. This is his festival not his funeral, right?

"Absolutely."

"So, why are we standing here?"

"Let's go." Theo encouraged.

We walked over to Duval Street, slid between the participants in the parade, pushing our way through the crowd about a block down to Charles Street and stopped at Perry's front door. We walked in without knocking.

Theodore called out, "Perry! Are you decent? We've got company."

Perry's voice was weak yet clear as it came from the bedroom. "Who's there?"

"It's Jay."

"I'm in the bedroom. Come on back."

Theodore and I made our way back to Perry's bedroom where he had a bunch of pillows stacked behind him so he could sit up and read. He put down his book and looked up at us.

Theodore began. "I told Jay that you weren't feeling

well, but he just insisted on coming over. I hope that was okay with you. I know you wanted to rest and all."

"That's fine, Theo," Perry interrupted. He turned to me and said, "Hi, Jay."

As I entered the room, Perry continued, "I know Theo talked you into coming back with him."

"Well, that's not entirely correct. I talked him into coming here with me. He wanted to let you just lie here and die."

"Bull!"

"Really. I just feel bad that you're missing the celebration you helped to plan. You're the honorary chairman of the whole thing. And you're just lying here."

"Well, this old body doesn't always do what I want it to do, you know; the disease and all."

"Enough excuses. Sometimes we feel better if other things in our lives are under our control like going out and having some fun."

"That's a nice attitude to have. But--"

"So, I'm here to take you out in the fresh air. It'll do you good."

"I'm trying to get well, Jay, not speed up the death process."

"Tell me, Perry. If you go out and enjoy yourself, will the disease get worse?"

"I don't know."

"So, let's assume the worst and say you're going to die. Okay? You might as well get the most out of every minute before it happens. Right? If you're not going to die, then what the hell does it matter what you do? So, let's go party."

"I never could win an argument with you."

"Theo, pick him up and let's go."

"I can walk to my chair. I'm not one hundred percent handicapped."

"No, sir," Theo interjected, "The doctor told you not to walk. I'll put you in the wheelchair."

"No! Don't!"

"No argument. You hear me?"

Theodore picked up Perry and weaved his way through the apartment and placed him into the wheelchair with a gentle hand. He pushed Perry and the chair to the front door where I held it open for them, acting like the Queen's Footman at Buckingham Palace.

We exited out the back way of Perry's house which opened onto Telegraph Lane. We crossed the street and walked up Charles to Duval where the crowd parted to allow Perry through to watch the parade for a while.

Many of the folks in the crowd greeted Perry, each making a big fuss over the fact that he was out and smiling. One young man dressed in drag stopped and gave Perry a great big kiss on the lips and shouted "Wow! Perry Savant is still my favorite man," and walked on.

Perry looked back at the young man walking away and Theo said to him, "Stop staring, dear. I'm mad enough as it is since you let that hussy kiss you like that."

"Theo, you're the only one who can do that and make me like it."

Theo straightened up a little more and began to smile picking up the pace a bit then added an aside meant for me, "I just love to tease him and make him compliment me."

As Perry sat watching the various floats move by, many of the people on the floats saw him and yelled out their good wishes. Some even threw him kisses and handfuls of candy which he attempted to catch.

Several little children standing nearby ran over to Perry and picked up the candy to hand to him. However, each time someone did, he closed the young person's hand over the candy and told them to keep it since he's not supposed to eat that kind of stuff.

After about an hour, Perry turned to Theo and said he'd like to move through the crowd rather than sit because he was feeling restless. We all laughed and moved on down Duval Street toward the Ta-Da Club where we stopped. It was about eight forty-five p.m.

Perry asked, "What are we doing here?"

"Well, you missed Brian's big show last Saturday at the opening party," Theo told him. "You were too sick then. So, I've decided that you're not going to miss his grand premier tonight of his latest song and character."

"I hadn't heard about that."

"This new act of Brian's has been a major secret. I don't even know what he's planning to do. And you know he tells me almost everything."

"How are we supposed to get a table? Look at that line of people?"

"You're talking to a good friend of the headliner here. I've reserved a front row table just for the three of us. Plus, Brian promised that he'd come join us after the act is over."

Perry smiled and shook his head in surrender and said, "Let's go."

Nine

Nine PM, Saturday, October Thirty-first

THE EVENTS IN THE FOLLOWING description contain some speculation, but I have tried to piece together what I believe happened while we sat in the Ta-Da Club awaiting Brian's big show.

‡   ‡   ‡

IT WAS SATURDAY NIGHT, Halloween, and Fantasy Fest: these three elements would seem to almost anyone to be a perfect prescription for horror; but, then this is Key West, and that combination of factors is considered to be a perfect prescription for an amazing week-end party for the whole city! Well, except for one young man walking west on Greene Street headed toward Duval, that is. For him this night would be that moment in his life when everything would change. By early Sunday morning, he would become one of America's Most Wanted.

As thousands of people gathered along Duval Street for the biggest event of Fantasy Fest, the night sky enveloped that figure as he moved in such a way as to avoid the street lamps along his route. He stopped in the shadow of a large live oak tree a block short of the crowds that pressed upon the parade site.

The man in the shadows studied another person standing alone under a light pole. He recognized him as Brian Silver by the way he was dressed: in the fashionable elegance of a well-tailored suit with an expensive, stylish pin point oxford shirt and a rep tie that was folded into a perfect Windsor knot wrapped around his slim yet muscular neck. But there was that thing around his neck: Brian's trademark, as he would often refer to it whenever questioned.

Still lurking in the darkness of the massive tree spread above him, the dark figure realized that as he stood there staring at Brian his heart rate began to beat faster than normal. He could feel his stomach churn as if in serious need of a seltzer.

But at this moment his face became almost hot to the touch as he realized that he was not as prepared for this meeting as he had hoped he would be. He had not anticipated his own personal feelings about Brian who stood half-a-block away.

He looked at his watch. Nine-fifteen. "I'm late," he muttered almost out loud. Exiting the shadows, he moved at a quick pace down the block and stood within five feet as

Brian turned and spoke in a quiet voice, "You're late."

The words seemed to sting like an unexpected encounter with a wasp. All this man of the shadows could do was utter an almost unintelligible, "Sorry." Then as if snatched in mid-air, he wished he could take that word back and say something more interesting--or at least more original.

Brian said, "You didn't dress for the parade?"

"No. Didn't feel like it. You look your usual stunning self. I like the addition of the, uh, trademark?"

"Gotta keep up the image, you know."

"Image? Yea. Image."

There was a long pause.

Brian said, "So, are you ready?"

"I'll know in a minute."

"I hope you don't mind my saying this, but I've been a little worried about you lately."

"Why?"

"You've been late a lot. I mean for over a week. And just like tonight. I thought we were meeting at nine."

Hesitating for a moment, the man replied with a meek, "I know."

Brian stared at stared at him for several moments. Then with a sigh said, "Well, you asked for this meeting."

The dark man hesitated.

"Yeah, no, I mean, so, what do you say?"

Brian shook his head side to side and said, "I, really, I mean, can't we just be just..."

"Friends? Friends?"

"Why not?" Brian said as he smiled with an almost disarming charm that should have brought the other man from the darkness into the light of friendship. "Really. C'mon. Why complicate our relationship?"

"What relationship?" was the terse reply.

"You know, like, we're professionals. Why can't we just be colleagues and maybe good friends?"

"Professionals? I'm a professional. But you--"

"What?"

"Just forget it."

"C'mon. There's no need to get all huffy about it."

"Hell no. I'm done. You hear me? Done."

"Look, I never wanted any of this."

Brian's words froze in his mouth as a look of astonishment crossed his face. He looked down to see where the sting in his chest was coming from. He leaned back hard against the light pole. And with an expression of total disbelief he slid down the pole as if in slow motion and melted into a heap on the concrete.

The man from the shadows looked down at his hand in which he held a twenty-two calibre pistol with a small whiff of gun powder still rising from the barrel. With all the noise from the parade and the crowds, no one seemed to notice a gun shot. But, the barrel was so close to Brian's mid-section, it seemed to muzzle the sound.

Placing the pistol back into his pocket, he turned away and walked in the direction from which he had come down Greene Street. And a moment or two later, he disappeared into the darkness and away from Brian who was now sitting on the pavement under the street lamp a half-block from Duval Street.

After several minutes, a young man in the crowd

walked over to Brian and shouted, "Hey, mister, you okay?" When there was no response, he reached down and touched him. As he did, Brian fell backward from the light pole and onto the sidewalk. Although he only wanted to see what he could steal, he couldn't stop himself from yelling out, "Damn! I think he's; I mean; I think he's dead."

Just then another man dressed in casual slacks and open-collared shirt stepped over to see what was going on. When he noticed the man on the ground he reached over to check Brian's pulse. He turned to the other man with, "What have you done?"

"Nothing, mister. I swear. I mean I was going to lift his wallet, you know. I thought he was drunk. But, he's dead. I mean scared the hell out of me."

At this moment, several other people gathered and one even grabbed the would-be pick-pocket and held him tight.

"Don't let him go anywhere while I call the police," he said as he pulled out his cell phone and called 911.

‡ ‡ ‡

AT 9:38 P.M. THE POLICE dispatcher answered a call about a man who had been shot down on Greene Street half a block from Duval. However, the dispatcher, Emily Deshotel, believed the call was a prank and began to laugh. She knew about the five deaths in Key West during the past fifteen years

The low crime rate was used by the founders of Fantasy Fest to help make the annual Halloween celebration one of the fastest growing of its kind in the Americas. In addition to the crime rate, residents of this small town have a 'live and let live' attitude toward life; another reason why so many people who faced open opposition in many other parts of the country came to visit, and often stayed, in Key West.

The leaders of the week-long festival had claimed for years that during the celebration no one was ever injured, other than minor scrapes. In fact, the festival had never been marred by serious crimes at all in its more than twenty-year history.

So no one could blame Emily for not believing that the caller was serious. As a career police dispatcher, she had moved to work for the City of Key West after twenty years with the Miami-Dade 911 service. Her bright red hair was always set upon her head in a perfect swirl. Some of her colleagues believed she wore a wig, but the fastidious nature that kept her hair in perfect order wherever she went also made her one of the best 911 operators in the state of Florida.

After hitting the cough button so she wouldn't be overheard laughing, Emily looked up and called over to the desk sergeant sitting about ten feet from her.

"Sergeant, someone's reporting a murder on Greene Street."

"A murder? Now that's a new one."

"I mean, out of all the pranks I heard over the years, never a murder. Can you believe that?"

"Hey, it's Halloween. We get prank calls like that all the time."

"Maybe I should act like this is real and scare the person on the line."

"As much fun as that might be, I think you should just

get their information and tell them we'll have someone there when we get around to it."

"Okay. But you know, I think I'll call Pearson and check with him first. He's assigned parade duty in that area."

She picked up the walkie-talkie to call Wally Pearson, one of the mounted police officers patrolling the parade. However, Pearson's voice crackled through on the radio receiver before she could make her call.

"Dispatch, this is Mounted Three. Show me 10-51 at Greene Street and Duval. I have a 10-46 reported behind Sloppy Joes Bar. Possible Signal 5 requesting 10-24."

As if turning on like a light switch, Emily responded to Pearson's call and sent out a call for all available officers to respond to Duval and Greene Streets for a possible homicide. She called for an ambulance to the location, lights and siren authorized. After taking a deep breath, she turned back to the other caller and assured him that help was in route.

Although quite nervous and embarrassed at her first response, Emily knew what to do once she had ascertained that a true emergency had occurred. The department held a practice drill a week earlier for a possible emergency in order to prepare for the festival events.

The emergency response drill included all police, fire, water and electric as well as other service and maintenance workers. All were given refresher courses in CPR and reminded of their responsibilities to public safety.

‡   ‡   ‡

OFFICER PEARSON LOOKED impressive as he sat in the saddle high atop his sixteen-hand tall brownish steed. Unlike most of the other Key West police officers who wore open collared golf shirts with embroidered badges, Pearson always wore his dress uniform with a starched white shirt and jet black tie. The badge pinned on the just-pressed coat shone like a spotlight from his chest. He always seemed to strike just the right pose for camera-happy tourists at all times. He considered himself within the finest tradition of mounted officers such as those in Chicago, New York, and London.

Pearson moved through the crowd toward the site of the shooting with little difficulty. As soon as he turned off Duval and onto Greene, he guided his horse in such a manner as to move through the crowd to the spot where the victim was lying on the ground.

Upon arrival he attempted to ease the onlookers away from the victim who was lying at the base of a streetlamp. He looked down at the young man and was struck by the way he was dressed. He could see that the man was not dressed as everyone else but had on a well-tailored, expensive suit, pink shirt and tie. This was out of context for Fantasy Fest. Most of the people in the parade and in the crowd were dressed in all sorts of costumes at various stages of undress.

Pearson noticed that the young man's chest was moving as he gasped for breath. Shaking himself out of his shock, Pearson dismounted and fell to his knees, grabbed a handkerchief from his own pocket, and placed it on the wound in the middle of the man's chest.

A quite youthful face looked up at him and offered the faint trace of a smile. Pearson realized that the man looked very familiar, but he felt troubled since he couldn't place him. As he gazed into the man's eyes, he realized that tears were starting to stream down his own face.

This was the first time he had been in this situation other than in training exercises. Although he had never done it before in an actual emergency, he attempted to stop the bleeding by applying pressure just as the instructors explained in their classes. Despite his effort he watched the young man below him smile and close his eyes.

"Stay with me, sir. Keep your eyes on me. Look at me. You're going to make it," Officer Pearson pleaded as he held the handkerchief tight against the bleeding wound. He whispered a prayer or maybe it was a desperate plea for help as he said, "Please, God! Help him!"

Unaware that a fire rescue vehicle had just arrived along with two patrol cars from the police department, Officer Pearson continued trying to save the life of the man he thought couldn't be more than thirty years old.

"We'll take it from here," an EMT said in a soft yet firm voice to the policeman. He placed his hand over the officer's to signal him to pull his hand away which he did with a slow, careful motion.

The other two paramedics were already at work talking to the man and attempting to keep him alive. Officer Pearson stepped back, knowing in his heart that their work was in vain. He had felt the life drain from the victim's body and watched the spark of life leave his eyes.

Pearson felt the tears rolling down his cheeks as he

leaned against the auburn colored steed that was as dear to him as any friend he had ever known. He removed his well pressed, black uniform jacket and placed it over the saddle. He loosened his tie, unbuttoned his shirt, and used his sleeve to wipe away the tears that flowed in a steady stream from his eyes. He could not understand what had just happened. He had tried so hard, but was unable to save the life of the young man on the ground.

One of the EMT's removed the tie and shirt from the victim's neck and chest. He also removed the red scarf from around his neck. With a spark of understanding and recognition he signaled to Pearson and said, "I think this might be important. You'd better take possession of it." The EMT offered the boa to the officer who reached over and took it and placed it under his arm.

"Thank you," Pearson said as he continued to dry his eyes. As he focused on the item in his hand, his first thought may have been, Why didn't I notice this when I was holding the handkerchief over the wound? He pulled a small notebook from inside his coat pocket and began jotting down notes about what had just happened. He heard the sounds of several police cars pulling up to the scene. The detectives had arrived.

Pearson continued to stand leaning against his horse for several minutes making sure that the EMT's were not disturbed as they placed the man on a gurney and lifted him into the back of the ambulance and sped away with lights flashing red and white.

One of the bystanders clad in yellow and purple paint and only a loin cloth that barely covered his vitals said to the officer, "Hey! Wasn't that?" Pearson raised his hand to stop the rest of the spectator's sentence and said, "There will be no official statements at this time. Please do not spread rumors."

Several uniformed officers pushed people back and put up police investigation tape and other barriers to keep the onlookers out of the crime scene. As a detective approached Officer Pearson, he bowed his head and said, "I tried my best. I've never felt so helpless. I just couldn't help him."

The detective attempted a comforting thought, "Wally, the man was already dead when you got to him. The vic seems to have bled out quickly. There was nothing anyone could do."

The officer looked up and told the detective, "You'll need this," as he handed him the boa taken from the dead man. "The EMT's took it from around the victim's, uh, Brian's neck."

He handed the detective the small notebook he had been writing in. "And here are my notes of what happened when I arrived. I need to get down Duval and catch up with the crowd. They've probably already reached Truman Avenue. I need to get there and help keep people..."

Pearson gulped then wiped the tears from his eyes again.

The detective reached over and placed his hand on Wally's back as he called for another detective to bring him a large evidence bag. The other detective grabbed one from out of the trunk of their cruiser then held it open so the detective could drop the boa into it. He sealed the bag, labeled it, and signed the front of the clear plastic bag. The detective leaned over to Pearson and said, "I'm sorry, Wally, but you need to put your signature on the next line here."

Pearson signed the bag. Then raised his head and dried his tears with his shirt sleeve which was already wet from tears and sweat.

"You go on back to your duties." The detective said. "We'll talk tomorrow."

Officer Pearson buttoned his shirt, tightened his tie, put on his jacket, lifted himself onto his trusty steed, rode the hundred feet or so to Duval Street and turned south.

The detective looked down at the item Pearson had handed him and studied it through the clear plastic. With a spark of intense recognition, his eyes widened as he uttered out loud, "Oh, no! Not Brian!"

Ten

Ten PM, Saturday, October Thirty-first

THE NIGHTCLUB WAS PACKED full of people dressed in all sorts of costumes and various stages of undress. Transvestites stood everywhere. Two young men sat very close to each other involved in serious kissing as several older couples who looked like tourists seemed a bit flustered by all that was going on.

One elderly couple in particular acted as if this was the kind of thing they'd been doing all their lives; yet, their eyes betrayed just how uncomfortable they were even though they tried their best to appear relaxed.

Perry, Theodore, and I entered following Ruthie who came out to the front herself to escort her friends to the central front row table. As we were seated, two performers in drag were just finishing their number as applause exploded all over the room.

As the performers left the stage, Perry leaned over to me and said, "These guys are really good."

I countered, "Everyone who performs here is terrific. It's been a long time since you last attended a show here. And I mean I can't believe you don't come more often to enjoy the exceptional entertainment."

"I can't remember the last time we were here, either" said Theo. "I've never seen those ladies before."

Seeming to be the expert, I stated with a tone of authority, "The blonde's name is Adrienne Herbert. He arrived here around the first of July. I think he's from Virginia by way of Atlanta."

Perry chimed in with, "He's good. When is Brian doing his thing?"

"He's the star of the show and will be the climax at the end of the ten-thirty show."

"God, I've been out of circulation a long time. I didn't know. I knew he had become quite popular, but the star?"

"Perry, you've had more important things to worry about rather than who's performing at the Ta-Da club."

"I know. But, I like to keep up with what's going on. So when does that world famous band of Ruthie's start playing again?"

"They'll be playing the entire ten-thirty performance. Ruthie had them pre-record music for these warm up acts prior to the big show."

Just then I noticed Ruthie walking up onto the stage. The audience noise quieted as she made her way to center stage.

She approached a microphone that a stage hand had placed on the stage only moments before she arrived. She stood there for several moments that seemed like hours. I leaned over to Perry and whispered, "Something's wrong. Ruthie never introduces the acts. She has a manager who does the introductions over the public address system."

Ruthie took a deep breath and started to speak, but stopped, and turned away. Pausing to wipe her eyes with several tissues in her hand, she turned back to the microphone and spoke in a slow and distinct voice as the tears started to roll down her cheek.

Reading from a prepared statement, Ruth said, "Ladies and gentlemen, I'm sorry to have to announce that due to circumstances beyond our control our headliner, Brian Silver, will not be performing as scheduled tonight."

There was a great rumbling in the audience in reaction to the news. People expressed their extreme disappointment.

Ruth raised her hand and waited for the crowd to calm down. She continued, "There's been a shooting near Sloppy Joes just down the street. The police have responded and are now investigating what happened. The chief just called me to report that the person shot has been identified as Brian Silver."

We sat in stunned silence along with the rest of the people in the room. Several gasps could be heard as people got up and left. Performers stood just off to the side of the stage crying as Ruth walked over to console them.

Perry reached over and took Theo's hand as tears rolled down both men's cheeks.

I sat stunned only able to utter, "My God."

Perry looked over at me, his face now turned hard as nails. His years of NYPD experience and training aided him as he began to formulate some thoughts about the future. He spoke in a solemn tone, "This is going to get nasty. Things are going to be tough for the next several days, maybe even months."

I nodded in agreement as I said in a soft voice, "I hope to God you're wrong, my friend. I hope you are wrong."

We sat looking down at our drinks and the table. I had no words. So, I decided to do something. I stood. "I'm going down there and see what's going on."

"Wait," Perry said, "You can't be of any help. The police will have the whole area cordoned off."

"I know. But, I can get some details from the investigators so I can report back to you about it."

I walked out.

‡   ‡   ‡

ABOUT SIX BLOCKS AWAY on Duval Street, the scene was chaotic. As I walked toward Greene Street, I noticed that Sloppy Joes Bar had all but emptied out as people tried to get a glimpse of the horrific scene just outside the famous landmark. As I turned onto Greene, I could see through the crowd where Brian's body had been. A chalk outline on the sidewalk marked the spot.

The police tape and barriers held back the crowd. People stood nearby, shocked and dismayed at what had happened. Murders were rare in Key West. Not a single person of any note was ever murdered, especially someone as famous as Brian. I could hear People asking each other, "Who could do such a thing?" And others whispered, "Some people just hate fags."

Only a few minutes passed when the crowd cleared the area. Celebrating had stopped and the streets appeared deserted long before midnight. One young man wearing only a pair of tight spandex briefs walked over to the scene, stopped at the police tape. He looked down at the pool of blood that seemed to have formed the shape of Brian's body on the cement, the chalk marking still visible where the blood had not covered it. He looked down at his right hand which held a bouquet of wild flowers. He tossed the spray so that it landed next to the hallowed ground. With a tear-stained face, he said, "Good bye, Brian."

I wandered around the area talking to people since the police were not saying anything at all. It seems that no one saw what happened. A moment or two later, I saw a new friend, our city's police chief, Fatima Sax.

I think she never expected to be looking over a scene like this when she accepted this promotion. But, it did not take her long to understand the gravity of this situation, so she appointed her best detectives to investigate nothing else until this case was solved.

David Hernandez, Key West's chief of detectives, headed up the task force that was made up of Key West Police detectives, special investigators from the Sheriff's office, and a representative from the Florida Department of Law Enforcement. I was told that their job was to piece together just what happened on Greene Street that

Halloween night.

"Chief," I called out. She looked toward me and signaled for me to join her near the crime scene behind the yellow tape.

As I walked up, Detective Hernandez spoke. "What a waste," He had accepted the position of chief of detective for the city almost a year to the day. He worked as a detective for the Monroe County Sheriff's office for more than fifteen years, so he knew his stuff. Even though he was known as a man of few words, he brought a practical perspective to every investigation. Fatima told me several years later that she learned early to appreciate his skills and discretion.

She answered him. "I don't know, Dave, perhaps this happened for a reason. Maybe our department needed to be forced into the twenty-first century with a case that would force us to upgrade our equipment and skills."

Hernandez stood there making notes in the little black book he carried with him everywhere. Fatima looked over at him waiting for the response that often never came unless the answer was so important that he felt compelled to speak. People often referred to him as the "gentle giant" because of his impressive size of 260 pounds on a frame of 6'3" in height.

She hinted for a comment as she said, "Don't you think so?"

"Probably," Hernandez stated in an off-handed way.

"What do you think happened here?"

"Somebody shot him," Dave quipped as he continuing to write in the notebook.

Fatima looked at him with a smile. Although she

appreciated his frankness, she still attempted to engage him in conversation every chance she could; but every effort ended to no avail. Since they first met, she wondered just how he was able to stay married for so long with such minimal conversational skills. Then she met his wife at a department picnic. What rolled over and over in her mind after that encounter was, *does this woman ever shut up?*

Fatima let out a small chuckle evoking a response from Hernandez.

"What?"

Caught off guard, Sax said, "Sorry. I was just thinking about something else. Actually, I'm thinking that we may need a lot of help on this one."

"Yep."

"I'll call the Sheriff first thing in the morning and get their detectives in here to help you out."

"Okay."

"And I think maybe we might need a bit of undercover help here as well. What do you think?"

"Whatever you think, Chief."

"You finish up here, Dave. I need to take care of a little business near here. I'll come back and get my car in about a half hour."

"Okay," he responded without looking up. He walked over to another detective and started to talk to him.

Fatima turned to me and said, "You might be interested in this. I'm headed over to talk to Perry. Want to join me?"

"Yes!" I answered with enthusiasm.

We walked past Sloppy Joes and crossed Duval Street, and walked to Charles and the alley leading to Perry's house. We stopped at the wrought iron gate and pushed the button on the call box to the right of the gate. The little speaker sounded out.

"Who is it?"

"Fatima Sax. Oh, and Jay is with me."

"Come on in," was the reply as the buzzer sounded and the gate opened automatically. We entered into the courtyard and to the front door where Theo greeted us with a hug and tear-reddened eyes.

"He's on the back patio. Oh, and he's expecting you."

Fatima shook her head with a smile and walked out onto the patio area where Perry was seated in his favorite spot under a huge banyan tree that gave tremendous shade from the daytime sun and some protection from the evening dew.

"Perry, how are you feeling?"

Perry shifted with a grimace and turned to see us walking toward him.

"I feel like crap, Fatima. How do you feel?"

"Emotionally? Probably the same, but fine physically."

"And how are you, Jay?"

I nodded my courtesy and found a place to sit down.

"So, to what do I owe this honor?" Perry encouraged.

"I thought you would have already thought that question through and anticipated my arrival."

"You don't think it was a hate crime, do you?

"Honestly? I don't know what to think about this one."

Perry stared at her. "So, what is it that brought you to my place so late at night?"

Fatima let out a deep sigh and sat next to Perry.

"Here's what we've been able to discover in just a few

hours. He was shot up close. There was obvious stippling all around the wound and on his clothing. No one noticed anything unusual going on, so they don't appear to have been arguing or shouting or anything like that. Brian must have known his attacker and felt no threat at all. Also, there have been no indications from our office, the sheriff's office or even FDLE as to any threats by terrorists or anti-gay groups."

"So you think this may be a simple case of passion or perhaps revenge?"

"I don't know. You're the man with all the experience with this type of crime. How about helping us out here?"

Perry looked into Fatima's eyes. "You're holding something back," he said. "Something else has happened?"

"Before I had gotten my stuff together to go out to the scene, the switchboard got calls from ABC, NBC, and FOX who all wanted to know what was going on in Key West. Then I got a call from the Sheriff himself. He was upset. Videos and pictures of the crime scene were all over the internet and on the eleven o'clock news. People were calling for an investigation into what the media was calling a hate crime."

"People are already saying it's a hate crime?"
"Yes."

"I'd be angry as hell if I were you," Perry blurted out.

Fatima laughed. "Yea. I know. The real problem is that my hands are now tied. I'll be under tremendous scrutiny during these next several weeks. I'll be pressured into having my detectives investigate only the hate crime angle. I can't even risk asking the sheriff and his detectives to investigate anything other than that. And FDLE? Well, I wish I didn't have to get them involved at all, if it were my call. That might bring the governor down here."

"Fatima," Perry interrupted. "I'd be honored to snoop around behind the scenes and see what I can find out. I know you want to keep this thing local."

"Thanks, Perry. You're a dear. Oh, you might want this."

She handed him one of Brian's calling cards with something written on the back.

"He told me once that if anything happened to him, that I should call that person at that address in Miami. There's no phone number and it appears she doesn't have a cell phone in her name."

"Who is this 'Maria Hernandez'?

"I don't know. See if you can find out."

"Glad to do it."

"Great. I think I'll see if I can get a couple of hours of sleep before all hell breaks loose in the morning."

"Hell?"

"I expect an invasion of television trucks and hordes of reporters coming in here by daylight."

"Oh, there is one thing," Perry said. "I'll need to bring someone in to help me because of--."

"Yeah, I know. Who were you thinking of?"

Perry looked at Fatima as his face lit up with a smile.

Eleven

SUNDAY MORNING, I was sitting at my usual table at the Monument Street Café staring at the blank page in front of me. Even though I sat through the eight-thirty worship at the little Baptist church near my house, I found no comfort or consolation. I can only say that I was in a total state of disbelief; perhaps denial.

I stared out the window at the people passing by. I sipped on a cup of coffee and picked at my breakfast. I couldn't decide whether I was hungry or just plain sad. My thoughts wandered in all sorts of directions. After fifteen years of disciplined effort I was now unable to control my mind.

After several minutes my thoughts inched their way

back to the early days of adulthood. I had graduated Emerson College in Boston, an achievement not normal for the son of a shopkeeper from upstate New York. And like most young men in my predicament, I got my start as a cub reporter on a small newspaper near my home.

But my dream was to be a novelist. Since my dad paid the tuition to Emerson, I did not major in creative writing, I earned a journalism degree. Dad owned a store for more than thirty-five years and was a member of the parish of the local Episcopal Church. He supported my talent, but he also reminded me that I needed to support myself and a family.

The editors of the Binghamton Sun-Press did not set any specific times for me to be in the office. They required me to find good stories, write interesting articles, meet deadlines, and be ready to move on an assignment at any time day or night. So every evening I would sit on the front porch of the boarding house where I stayed and worked on my fiction with the wireless phone on the table in front of me in case a call came in to cover some breaking news. All they required of me was to be available 24/7.

One of my favorite topics in college was history. Thus, the articles I wrote for the paper were peppered throughout with historical references making them fun to read (at least in my opinion). It seems that my love of history also explains why my first three novels were so steeped in historical facts from the mid to late nineteenth century. The reviewers commented that the books made them feel as if they were watching the events as they occurred before their eyes.

The first book was a diplomatic mystery involving a character who worked as an assistant clerk for Prince Albert before he became the husband to Queen Victoria. I used Evelyn Anthony's book, Victoria and Albert, as my guide and reference source.

And since I was also a devoted follower of Agatha Christie, Charlotte Bronte, Charles Dickens, and Arthur Conan Doyle, I had a solid grasp of the historical settings of the Victorian period. I think readers could tell that I longed for the simpler days of that time.

I completed the final draft near the end of my third year as a reporter and sent off query letters to twenty publishers in hopes that one might pick up the book. In the letter, I explained that I was working on two more books like the first. Less than a year later I completed the second novel. As I was nearing the completion of the third I got a call from a publisher offering me an advance for the three books. I signed the contract on February 3 in the middle of a massive winter storm.

I received the check four weeks after signing the contract. That's the same day that I packed my bags, called the editor, quit my job, and hopped a bus to New York City. There I transferred to a train bound for Miami.

My family was concerned about my quick, almost hysterical, move in the middle of winter. Some people even speculated about a love affair gone bad, or that I was in debt to some gangster, or that I may have made the wrong people mad.

But no one, other than my father, ever called me or attempted to ask why I moved to Key West. On the other hand, I knew that I could not handle the winters any longer and thus never regretted leaving the bone-chilling cold of my hometown area.

When I left I knew that my father would sit back in the rocking chair that I had bought for him after he sold his store to a large chain of grocers and take life easy. I knew that the chair was the perfect thing to give to a man who was ending a thirty-five-year career on his feet. He could now sit in that chair and enjoy his life.

I also knew that Dad and Mom were both proud of my achievements, although my father never mentioned them or ever showed the least bit of pride in his son. I could deal with that since we understood each other.

Over the next five years, I would take the short flight to Miami twice a year and board a Jet Blue flight to New York. There I would rent a car and drive through the countryside to visit my parents during the spring and fall. Unfortunately, four years after his retirement my father passed away of a heart attack. He left my mother with an excellent income from investments he had made over the years.

After the reading of the will, we found out that rather than spending his money on his family, he invested it and made a fortune. It didn't take long to convince my mother to start traveling and see all of the things she would talk about but never had the money to do.

Although I rarely talked about my parents after leaving, deep inside I loved and cared for them both. Two years after my father died, my mother passed away leaving me with enough income to be a full-fledged citizen of Florida with no ties outside the state.

Now ten years after arriving in Key West, most of the permanent residents of Key West look upon me as an oddity since I wasn't gay and attended church almost every Sunday at a little Baptist church not too far from my house.

The talk around town was that I was in the closet and had moved to Key West where I would be left alone no matter what I was. Since I had brought good publicity to my new home with the books I wrote, two of which were New York Times bestsellers, few people cared what I did or what was my sexual orientation. Besides, this was Key West — the "live and let live capital" of the world.

Although raised in the Episcopal Church, I had little time for church during college. But, while serving as an intern in New York City, I worked with the producer of a program featuring Bart Barton who was known as the Howard Stern of local New York City television.

I spent most of my time running errands and typing up scenarios for the daily hour-long program. The producer was a woman named Jackie Margolis. I loved working with her because she was so open about teaching me all the secrets of writing for television.

She made a huge impression on me because she was not ashamed to speak about her religious faith. She was a member of a local Baptist church in Manhattan near her apartment. Well, I had been on the set for three weeks when Jackie invited me to go to church with her. I just had to accept, more for the opportunity to spend time with this beautiful, fascinating woman than for religious reasons.

For the next six weeks, I attended regularly and decided that the Baptist denomination was what I was looking for in a church affiliation. So I joined the church and moved my membership to Trinity Baptist Church in Boston when I returned to college.

After moving to Binghamton, I became a regular attendee at the Downtown Baptist Chapel. I was active in the Sunday school and even sang in the choir. When I arrived in Key West, I sought out a local Baptist church to attend. Although my writing kept me too busy traveling to do more than attend worship services on Sunday mornings, I was a regular contributor to the church's finances, which did not go unnoticed by the pastor. He made sure to call me or come by my place at least once a month to check up to see how I was doing.

So, I sat for over an hour, wondering about Brian's death and pondering just what was going on. Who could do such a thing? Why did this happen? The questions swirled in a cacophony of randomness in my brain with not one stopping long enough to be considered for an answer. If anyone saw me, it probably looked like I was staring into space.

"Jay?" My deep concentration was interrupted by a familiar voice.

"Oh. Hi Theo. What's up?"

"Perry sent me over to get you."

"He could have called me. He knows my cell number."

"I know, but he likes finding reasons to get me out of the house so I just don't argue about it anymore."

"Gotcha," I muttered then signaled for the waitress to bring my check.

"I didn't mean to make you stop. I mean you don't have to come this second."

"It's okay. You gave me a good excuse not to order

dessert. Besides, I can't seem to put anything on paper at this time."

"I think Perry will appreciate your coming without delay."

The waitress brought the check and took the twenty I handed her as I said, "Keep the change."

"Thank you, Mr. Morrison," she replied.

"Okay, Theo. Let's go."

We left the restaurant and walked together down Whitehall Street to Caroline where we turned right.

"This thing has hit the city hard," Theo commented, "Captain Tony's, Sloppy Joes, and even the Hog's Breath are all closed today."

We continued walking and turned onto Telegraph and headed down the deserted alley toward Perry's house. As we entered the back patio, Perry was sitting up in a lawn chair appearing more alert and in less pain than the night before. Perry looked up and smiled.

"Thank you for coming."

"When Key West's most famous resident calls, I come."

"I appreciate the vain attempt at a compliment, but I'm far from being anything other than a broken down old queen who's too weak to go to the toilet alone."

"Perry!" Theo and I both chided him simultaneously.

"Give it a rest, you two. When you can't take a dump by yourself, you're in pretty bad shape. I'm a realist."

"Okay, Perry. What's so important that you had to send someone to drag me over to your place?"

"Well, the investigation into Brian's murder may be a lot more complicated than anyone might have thought. After you left last night, I did some research on Brian and his entertainment past."

"Oh?"

"You don't know everything about me, Jay."

"I heard you were a cop or something like that."

"Actually, I was chief of detectives for NYPD. That was before their policy of don't ask, don't tell."

"You were outed?"

"Yes. And that ended my career. They decided to let me have my pension if I retired and moved out of state. Oh, and not make a fuss. They were afraid of the possible political and legal complications surrounding my retirement if the public found out. So instead of causing trouble with a big publicity raucous, I came here."

"That's terrible."

Perry raised his hand in recognition of my feeble attempt at sympathy.

"I'm glad it worked out this way. I thought I wanted to be a policeman forever; but I've enjoyed being retired and working whenever I wanted to. Over the years, I've helped the local police, the Miami-Dade PD, and FDLE."

"So, what does all this have to do with me?"

"As you know the chief wondered if I would help her with a special angle on the investigation."

"What does she think you can do that she can't?"

"Lots," Perry insisted, "She wants me to help her look for a possible motive and suspect outside the main investigation."

"Why?"

"Do you remember what she told me about the press

getting pictures and video?"

"Ah, yes. I remember."

"It's become a big deal. All the radio and TV networks and national papers have picked up on it and are insisting that this is a clear case of a hate crime against a gay man. The chief thinks I can quietly look at motives other than that particular one. She's concerned that if it's discovered that she or anyone on her staff or any of the detectives at the Sheriff's office are looking in other directions she'll be accused of trying to cover up the whole thing."

"But Brian wasn't gay."

"I know that. And you know that. But the news media don't know that. I would imagine they don't even want to know. Besides, what's Key West but the gay capitol of the world?"

"Does the chief suspect someone in the gay community?"

"Actually, she can't find any clues at this stage of the investigation. Nothing points to a clear-cut motive of any kind other than he was shot up close with a small caliber weapon. She wants to look into every possibility. But since the mayor, the press, and the sheriff are all watching everything she and her staff are doing, she thought I might be able to investigate other avenues outside the realm of a hate crime."

"I see. Has she looked into the Christian Center connection?"

"The what?"

"The Christian Center of Miami; the group that applied for the parade permit."

"Oh, yeah. That group. Definitely gay bashers," Perry

remarked.

"I believe there may be some sort of connection there. You know, that's where Brian used to go to church when he lived in Miami."

"I've been casually aware of Brian's connection to a church. How is that relevant to this case?"

"I'm not sure of anything, of course, but when I asked Brian about the pastor in relation to what you had talked to me about earlier this year, he was evasive. I'll bet there's something big there, especially since that pastor and some of his people are in town holding a big tent revival during Fantasy Fest. And I heard that the Miami paper printed something to that effect the morning of the first tent meeting."

"That's an interesting angle. It also explains why Brian was so upset that the group had applied for a parade permit. Remember when he was at the committee meeting several months ago? I'll do some asking around and see what I can discover from my point of view."

"So, what do you need from me?"

Perry raised his hands indicating his condition and said, "I can't get around anymore like I used to. So, I want you to be my feet and eyes."

"Why me? What about Theo?"

"Well, that's nice of you to think of Theo, but he's got his hands full just taking care of me, you know, wiping my ass."

"But, why are you asking me to help you. I'm not a detective."

"First, everybody around here knows and trusts you. Second, you're an excellent researcher. And last, I trust you."

"Perry, I do literary research, not investigations."

"What do you think investigating is?"

"But I'm no expert in evidence collection or criminal investigative techniques. Remember the last time you asked me to help you?"

"Look, just bring everything you find or hear to me, no matter how trivial. I'll put it all together and try to make sense of it."

I sat stunned, even bewildered for several moments. Perry looked at me and I guess realized that I was having serious second thoughts about it all and that he'd be putting me at some risk. It seemed odd, but I swear that deep down Perry knew I was the only person who could move throughout the community talking about Brian without drawing attention.

Perry leaned over and whispered, "There might be a good novel in it."

"That did it. You've got me."

"Good. Now what I need you to do is to talk to some of Brian's friends."

"What do I tell them?"

"I don't know. Maybe just tell them you're, uh, helping me put together, a, um, tribute to Brian's memory. Yes, that's it: a tribute for the newspaper."

"But that's a lie."

"Not really. You'll probably write a story for the newspaper before you turn it into a novel, right?"

"Probably."

"And you'll make it sort of a tribute to the life of Brian Silver, wouldn't you say?"

It didn't take me but a second to see where Perry was going with his thoughts.

"Obviously," I muttered with a sideways smile on my face.

"I'll call Phil at the newspaper to ask you to do it so that it isn't a lie. Besides, half of detective work is getting people to talk, even if you have to lie to them to get them started."

"Okay, I can do that."

"Sometimes you have to use a few half-truths to prime the pump."

"Okay. I'll do it on one condition."

"No cover-ups?"

"No cover-ups. No matter where it leads?"

"No matter where it leads. I guarantee. I want to see Brian's killer brought to justice just as much as you do. Maybe more."

"What if--"

"It's someone in the community? Well, we need that information for our own protection, don't we?"

"So where do I start?"

"I understand he may have had a girlfriend or a lady friend of some kind."

"You mean the card that the chief gave you?"

"She believes everyone in town thought he was gay. I mean, you can't fool people for very long into thinking you're gay when you're not. Most of us have known he was straight for quite a while. We just didn't care."

"I knew he wasn't gay, but I wasn't sure anyone else knew it."

"He was a great guy. We all loved him for who he was,

not for what he wanted us to think he was."

"Even though he wasn't gay?"

"You're not gay, either," Perry reminded me with a slight smile in his eyes.

"Touché."

"So, you might want to start with her. I believe she lives in Miami. I'm not sure, but I think she's Cuban. Do you speak Spanish?"

"Poco."

"Good. Try Little Havana." Perry reached into a drawer next to him and pulled out the calling card with the name and address written on it that the chief had given him the night before. "Her name is Maria Hernandez. I think you'll find her or someone who knows her at this address."

I took the card, pulled out my wallet, and put it in there for safe keeping.

"I'll get on it today. Anything else?"

Perry leaned forward and looked at me eye-to-eye and said, "Just be careful."

"I will," I said as I turned and walked out of the house and down Charles to Duval. I stopped and looked around at the emptiness of the street; and all the trash. Several city workers were busy attempting to clean the mess.

As I strolled along with my thoughts banging around in my head with no obvious order, I was struck by the almost complete lack of traffic. It was nearly lunch time, yet Wendy's was empty. I walked past Walgreens and saw two of the clerks standing out front smoking and looking bored. I noticed that Willie T's outdoor tables stood empty. So, I walked further down to the Ta-Da where I saw a small sign on an easel in front that stated, "Closed in honor of our beloved Brian."

Standing across the street from the Ta-Da Club I also noticed a large poster that was still on the wall outside advertising Brian's Barbara act. My thoughts went back to the night Brian had introduced his rendition of Barbara by performing her most famous song, "People."

He had introduced a new generation to the melodic tones of one of the great vocalists of the late twentieth century. Brian's voice sounded almost as clear and melodic as his musical idol. I often remember that as the last tones flowed from his mouth and the audience rose in a standing ovation, I could swear I saw tears rolling down Brian's cheek.

Okay, Jay. Get a grip. I chided myself. You can't spend so much energy mourning over your friend. The only thing you can do now is focus on helping Perry find his killer. And then you can write an appropriate tribute to a man who had brought a new excitement and joy to thousands of people's lives.

As I continued walking toward home, I stopped every so often and picked up some trash and carried it to a trash can. The irony of the tons of trash and the absence of people hit me hard. All this trash. So easy to find and throw away. Yet finding the trash that killed Brian would be a difficult task at best.

With that thought, I dug in my emotional heels and made a vow then and there that I would let nothing keep me from helping Perry find Brian's killer no matter what.

Twelve

Wednesday, November Fourth

I COULD HAVE FLOWN to Miami and back for less money and time than it took me to rent a car and drive there. But I wanted to relax a bit and enjoy the drive up Highway One. I got a convertible and put the top down. The sunshine and the cool breeze along this highway that separates two large bodies of water is amazing.

The sky seemed to glow with an effervescent bluish hue all the way. And along several miles, I felt I could see all the way to Cuba. I had the radio blaring out the sounds of B. B. King, Eric Clapton, and my favorite Blues singer of all time, John "Too Cool" McCool.

As I drove into the Little Havana section of Miami, I reached into my pocket for the card with the address written on it that Perry had given me the day before. I pulled over to the curb and opened a map of Miami. Although I rented a car with a GPS locator, I just felt more comfortable looking at a map than looking up an address on the dashboard locator. I made several turns onto SW 23rd Avenue, saw the street I was seeking, and turned.

I drove by several buildings, rolled to a stop, parked the car, and got out. Several men and women were sitting on the stoops and porches outside the houses and buildings on the street. The people seemed to stare at me.

My thoughts raced. Was it so obvious that I did not belong in that neighborhood? It must be that I am so Anglo-looking that my discomfort with the surroundings was evident. I knew a lot about Hispanic culture, especially Cuban, because of my research. But, they knew I did not belong here.

I walked up to one of the doors and knocked. A beautiful young twenty-something lady leaned out of an open upper level window and looked down at me. She yelled in perfect English without even a whisper of an accent, "What do you want?"

"I'm looking for Maria Hernandez."

"Does she know you?"

"Probably not."

"Why do you want her?"

"That's for me to say to her alone."

"Que gringo tan estupido!" she said under her breath.

That's when I replied, "Tengo noticias de Brian."

"And how do you know Brian?" the girl questioned.

"He was my friend in Key West."

"Who are you?"

"Jay Morrison."

"Jay Morrison? Wait there. I'll be right down."

Maria drew herself from the window, ran down the stairs to the front entrance, and opened the door. She stepped out onto the porch and reached her hand to me.

"I'm Maria."

"I appreciate you seeing me."

"Brian talked a lot about you. He said that if anything happened to him I could talk to you without any fear."

"Is there someplace we can talk?"

"Sure. But not here."

"My car?"

Maria walked to the car and got in on the driver's side and said, "I'll drive."

I shook my head in disbelief then opened the passenger side car door and got in. Maria reached out her hand as I took the keys out of my pocket and handed them to her despite the fact that the rental agent told me not to let anyone else drive. She put the key in the ignition, started the car, and peeled rubber as we drove off.

We traveled east for a while, made several sharp turns to the right, and then left as if she was trying to lose anyone who may have been following us until we came to a deserted outdoor storage area under Interstate 95. She pulled around a building until the car was under the viaduct and turned the engine off.

As she turned to me, I said, "How long have you known Brian?"

"We went to high school together. We also attended the

same church."

"Christian Center?"

"Yes. You know about Pastor John?"

"I'm beginning to."

"If I were investigating Brian's murder, I'd start with him or at least his sidekick Marcus Champion."

"Why?"

"Because, there's a lot going on there they don't want people to know about."

"What in particular?"

"Like where does the money go? Or who's sleeping with whom? Or who's in charge over there?"

I sat waiting for more. There was a moment or two of silence. I asked, "There's something else? Isn't there?"

She turned her face away from me and paused in thought. She let out a sigh, turned her head back toward me.

"Look, I don't want to disparage anyone. And I'm not the kind of person that spreads rumors, but there seems to be something important going on."

"Just tell me. We'll sort it out."

"Okay, but remember that this is just a rumor. I don't know if it's true or not. I heard that Brian might be the illegitimate son of John Santos."

"Whew. That's big, especially for the pastor of a large conservative church."

"I know," she replied, "He never said anything about it himself and I never got up the courage to ask him after I heard it from someone in the church."

"That's okay. I'll pass this on to someone who'll be able to check it out and might even be able to figure out if it's the truth or not."

"Will you let me know when you find out?"

"Of course, I will. Now, what about Key West?"

"What about Key West?"

"He talked about people he knew. He mentioned me."

"Yeah, I know."

"So, who else did he talk about?"

"A man named Jerry or Perry, I think. Said I could trust him. And you, of course. He talked about you a lot. Says you were the only Christian in town he knew."

"Perry and I are working together on this."

"Good. Brian liked Perry. Said he was dying of AIDS?"

"He's the one who got me involved in this investigation."

"He also talked about a man named Theodore."

"Theo. Yes. He's Perry's life partner."

"That's what he called him. Said he was a straight arrow."

"Actually he's more like a limp noodle. But he's alright."

"Brian also talked about a lady named Ruth. I think she has something to do with the club where he performed."

"She owns the place. She's the one who talked him into coming to Key West."

"I used to hate him doing that."

"What?"

"Dressing like a woman and singing in front of people, you know? But he made so much money, I mean, what could I say?"

"Who else did he talk about?"

"Let's see, he mentioned someone named Harvey and someone named Sly or Clyde or Fly--"

"Styles?"

"Yeah. Styles."

That name caused me to pause a moment from a bit of shock. But I recovered with, "Did he say anything about him?"

"Not that I remember; maybe that he was so talented. I think Styles played in the band."

"Yes. That's right. Anyone else? Did he say anything about anyone else like in the band or the community?"

"I think he mentioned someone named Harvey as being an entertainer at Ruth's place. I don't remember about anybody else."

"Styles' real name is Karl Perkins. He's the pianist. Not many people know him or even call him by that nickname in Key West. Was there anyone else?"

"No. I can't think of anyone else. But, I think we'd better leave. That Miami-Dade Police Cruiser has passed by here three times now and is paying a little too much attention."

She started the car and moved back onto the street and drove back to her place. We rode silently until she pulled up and stopped in front of her building.

"Thank you, Maria," I said. "Here's my card. You can call me on my cell phone anytime if you think of anything else."

"I appreciate what you're doing. I loved Brian."

She opened the door and got out. As she closed the door she stopped.

"We were planning on getting married--next summer. Did he tell you that?"

"No," I uttered with a stunned look. "I'm sorry for your loss. I think he must have loved you a great deal. He was a true friend to me."

"Oh, I forgot. Just before he died, he called me and said that he had run into Marcus Champion in Key West. He seemed to be upset."

"About what?"

"He wouldn't tell me. He said he'd call me back when he took care of something he had to do. Oh, and he said that things like this have a way of working themselves out."

A tear began to roll down her cheek.

"I wish I had insisted that he talk to me more. I wish--"

"Maria, don't. There was nothing you could have done to stop what happened. Nobody could. Thousands of people were there when he was shot and no one was able to stop it."

"I know, Jay. I know."

"I appreciate your help."

Maria stood on the sidewalk as I slipped to the driver's side of the seat and started the car and said, "I guess I'd better start the long drive back."

"Oh, and Jay?"

"Is there something else?"

"Find Brian's killer. Please."

"We will."

It broke my heart, but I drove off leaving Maria on the corner as I noticed her mouthing the words, "Vaya con Dios."

‡   ‡   ‡

THE DRIVE BACK seemed long on that hot afternoon. As I bore to the right at Key Largo headed toward the east, I tuned the radio to a local station just in time to hear a report describing a three-car pile-up on the seven-mile bridge. I continued on anyway knowing I was about an hour from that bridge. I hoped that the wreck would be cleared up by then.

By the time I reached Islamorada, traffic was creeping along at ten miles per hour. Not fun for any of the people on the road that day. At one point where the road widened a bit, I pulled up next to a convertible driven by an attractive blonde. In the passenger seat sat a woman who seemed to be my age with her long brown hair tied back. So for the next ten minutes we chatted until the road narrowed again and the girls pulled out ahead of me.

Around the next bend I noticed a small hole-in-the-wall café I didn't remember ever seeing before. But being too tired to care what it looked like, I pulled off the road, gave up my place in line, and parked in front. After walking in, I looked around. I was alone, so I chose a booth, sat down and looked at the menu sitting on the table.

After about a minute a man walked in from the back and went behind a counter. He fit the stereotypical greasy spoon-type short order cook like that depicted in the Saturday Night Live skit "Cheeseburger, Cheeseburger." He was almost bald and wore a dirty paper chef's hat that looked like it was copied from a cartoon series. With a toothpick hanging out of the side of his mouth, he said, "Do you want anything to drink?"

To which I replied, "A large glass of water and a beer."

"We don't got any beer or alcohol here. Just soda."

"Okay," Jay mused, "How about a Diet Coke?"

"Just soda."

"Coke?"

"I'll git 'er fer ya."

I tried not to, but I smiled with amusement at the guy's responses.

Did he even know what constitutes soft drinks? I mean just how stupid can people be? I thought.

The man brought over a can of RC Cola and placed it down on the table.

"What're ya havin'?"

"What's good?"

"Well," the guy drawled, "I got some fresh ham back 'er. Would ya like a ham and Swiss on rye?"

"Okay, a ham and Swiss on rye is fine with me."

"What kinda cheese?"

"What?" I nearly spit not believing what I was hearing.

"What kinda cheese you want?" the man stuttered again.

"Swiss?"

"Swiss?"

"Uh, yeah."

"Okay," the guy said and wandered off into the kitchen area.

No wonder there are no cars parked here, I thought.

I stood up and started to go the bathroom when I noticed there were no signs as to where the restrooms were located.

I called out, "Hey! Where's the restroom?"

"Out back," the guy answered.

"Out back?" I muttered. You have got to be kidding. I

thought places like this went away decades ago from health violations.

I walked out of the café and around back as I thought, I'll bet the bathrooms still have signs that say, "Whites" and "Negros" on the doors. But my imagination could not prepare me for what I saw: there stood an actual operating outhouse.

My eyes began to water as I attempted not to laugh with hysteria. It was made of wood and had a half moon cut out near the top of the door. It seemed to be taken out of an early Earnest Hemingway novel. I couldn't stop myself wondering if Hemingway had used this outhouse himself.

What the hell am I thinking? I almost spoke as I jolted back to reality. What a stupid thought. I wondered if I was starting to compare myself to Hemingway. My body shuttered at the idiocy of that idea. But, then again--

Shaking off the insanity of my thoughts again, I remembered that my intention was to wash my hands rather than use the toilet, so I turned around and walked back into the café. The sandwich and a few chips and a pickle were sitting on a plate on the table. I sat down and picked up the sandwich. With a deep breath, I took a bite, and began to chew.

Not bad. Not bad at all, I mused and finished up the sandwich and warm soda. After sitting for several minutes, I called for the waiter again.

No one answered.

"Hello!" I yelled out. Not hearing a response, I walked back into the kitchen but didn't see anyone. That's when I noticed that the kitchen was spotless; as if it had never been touched by human hands.

Here's a mystery, I thought as my eyes roamed the empty room.

I walked back into the front, took out my wallet, pulled out a ten-dollar bill, and left it sitting on the cash register. Shaking my head with amusement at the whole experience, I walked out of the diner, got into the car and drove off.

The traffic jam had subsided and the sun was creeping down toward its ultimate destiny with the horizon. It would be dark before I got back into town, so I pulled out my cell phone and dialed Perry's number.

"Hello, Perry here."

"Hey, Perry, it's Jay."

"Where are you, man? I thought you'd be back by now."

"Big wreck. Got jammed up."

"You drove?"

"I'd rather not talk about it."

"Happens only when you're in a hurry, doesn't it?"

"Yeah."

"So," Perry began, "What did you find out?"

"Not a lot, despite the fact that the girl can talk."

"But, did she say anything at all that will help us with this case?" Perry pushed.

"I've got a lot of stuff written down in my notes. When can I drop by?"

"How far out are you?"

"Probably be back around seven-thirty or eight."

"Okay, why don't I meet you at the cafe in the morning around ten?"

"Sounds good to me. We'll talk in the morning," I said

and hung up.

I settled back in the car and set the cruise control. I reached over and turned up the radio and enjoyed the mellow sounds of B. B. King singing "The Thrill is Gone" flowing into the air. Turning up the volume a little higher, I spent the next hour or so of the drive thinking about just what I had learned and what it might mean to help find the murderer of my good friend, Brian Silver.

Thirteen

Thursday, November Fifth

I ARRIVED AT THE Monument Street Café early. I wanted to get breakfast and jot down additional notes on what I had discovered during my trip to Miami before Perry and Theo arrived at ten. I was so early that the door was still locked. But, in less than a minute, the manager opened up and said, "You're here early, Jay."

Acknowledging the manager's comments, I went to my usual table, sat down, and pondered the conversation with

Maria as I jotted down several things on the pad.

At about quarter to ten, Theo and Perry entered the café and made their way through the tables and chairs to where I was seated. As they approached, I stood and helped Theo get Perry's wheelchair into the limited space available.

We settled in and ordered some breakfast and coffee. I got a refill on my coffee as Perry started things off.

"Okay. Tell me everything you learned. And leave nothing out."

"Well, there's a lot more than I thought at first. But, I think the most important thing I learned is that Maria and Brian were pretty thick. She told me they were planning to get married next summer."

Perry looked at me with a serious look in his eyes. "That's not all, is it?"

"No. She said she had heard that Brian may have been Pastor Santos' love child back in Havana."

Perry pondered that for a moment then said, "Brian was the son of John Santos? That's interesting."

"That would explain a lot."

"It sure would. Son embarrasses pastor of large Miami church."

"What a story. I wish I had had that headline over my name as a reporter. That kind of thing would have made my career back in upstate New York."

"Have you confirmed it?"

"No. Not yet."

"That may be important. I'll look into it. What else did she tell you?"

"Well, I got the distinct impression that the people in the

church didn't like what he was doing down here. And, he didn't tell her very much about his life or the people he knew."

"I can understand that. Did she say anything about anyone in Brian's circle of friends and colleagues?"

The waitress brought Perry and Theo their food.

I waited until she was finished.

"Not really. She just said he mentioned me, you and Theo and a couple of members of the band. But other than that, she said he didn't talk much at all about what was going on down here. But I guess I don't blame him. This business of his was keeping them apart."

"Of course."

"So, what else can I do?"

"Well, I think you could do some nosing around for me here."

"Wait a minute, Perry. You're not going to make me the bad guy in this investigation, are you?"

"Heavens no. If anything, I'll make you a hero."

"How are you going to do that?"

"When the time comes, I'll see that you get a lion's share of the credit. That should launch you into a new area of writing pretty quick."

"Hum," I mumbled rubbing my chin trying to look like I was deeply concerned over what he was asking. I smiled and said, "I like that. So what do you want me to do?"

"Talk to Ruth. See what she knows."

"What do you want me to ask her?"

"Ruth knows a lot more than she's ever willing to let on. Just get her talking. Then pay careful attention."

"I'll do what I can. Is that all you need of me?"

"I think so. If you learn something you think is important, call me at that moment. Otherwise, we'll get together tomorrow."

"Okay, Perry. I think I'll walk down to the club and talk to Ruth. She'll be in the bar working on her books at this hour. So, she won't be too busy to talk."

I stood up and turned to Theo and whispered.

"Take care of him, Theo."

Theo smiled and gave me his hand. He turned and put his arm around Perry. "Sometimes I wonder which of us is taking care of whom?"

We all laughed together as I walked out of the restaurant toward Duval Street.

As I walked, I stopped several times along the way to greet people I knew. I would often take a little time with some because these people were good to me, and I loved and appreciated them all. Along the way I noticed Old Gravely sitting under "his" tree located just outside Jimmy Buffet's Margaritaville Restaurant. As usual, he held his hand out to the tourists who passed by.

No one knew how old he was. In fact, I don't know if he ever told anyone. He would just say, "I'm older than my shoes, and I've outlived my hair." Then he would tip his hat and reveal a head that showed a perfect example of male pattern baldness. And, of course, he would hold the hat upside down in his hand in a "how about a tip" sort of way.

Gravely always wore the same large-brimmed hat that was similar to the one that Indiana Jones wore in the movies, but not really. This hat actually helped to emphasize the greying hair that clung to the sides and back of his head.

I stopped and handed Gravely a five spot before he had a chance to tip his hat. He looked at the bill and said, "Wow, Mr. Morrison. Did you come into a fortune or something?"

I replied the same way I did every time the old man would say those words. "No, Gravely, I just thought you might need a little extra today. Oh, and don't forget to get some food; Okay?"

"Thanks, man. You're a scholar and a gentleman."

Of course, I knew that as soon as the bar opened inside, he'd be there buying a bottle from the bartender. He'd sit in the backyard and drink himself into a stupor.

Later one of the kitchen helpers would take him to a back room and let him sleep it off on a cot they kept back there. Actually, I had made arrangements with the managers to be sure he got at least one square meal each day. They would give that to him before they would hand him a bottle of not-so-high-octane booze. That simple gesture usually cost me about a hundred dollars a month.

And Gravely? Well, he seemed content to be on the streets without starving. I can't say for sure that I was helping him. But at least over the past several months, he had more color in his face. And he seemed healthier than when I first met him.

I tried to get him to stay at the local shelter once, but he refused. Said he didn't feel safe at those places. "Besides," he would say, "sitting on the sidewalk on Duval Street helps me feel at home, you know?" I guess it was familiar. I didn't understand it, but I didn't want to rob him of what little dignity he felt he had been free to do what he wanted.

Sometimes I wondered if I was doing the right thing or not. But, I didn't feel comfortable forcing my will on the old guy. He smiled a lot and often played the old beat-up guitar he carried around. And he could really play that thing. He often made it sing. I liked thinking that he was part of famous band, but just down on his luck. Maybe struggled with drugs. All I can say is that it's just the way the people are here in Key West. They look out for each other.

I smiled as I continued walking further down the street arriving a few yards from the Ta-Da Club. I took a deep breath, then walked toward the front entrance.

As I entered the open-air bar area, I saw Ruthie sitting at one of the tables working on her books. She sat in a big, over-stuffed rocking chair with a smaller table next to her. On it were lots of papers and accounting books precariously balanced in a way she could see it all at a glance.

The papers were being held down by various heavy objects that had been collected over the years from places she and her husband had visited. With the slight breeze blowing off the Florida Straits toward the Gulf, the pages were flapping and blowing as the weights barely held each item in its place.

I stopped a few feet from her and greeted her with, "That looks like exciting work."

"You want to do it for me?" she quipped.

"No thank you."

"So why the hell are you disturbing me?"

"Just visiting."

Ruthie cracked a big smile as she let out a huge laugh. "The hell you are, baby."

"Oh? Why am I here?"

"'Cause you been snooping around asking questions about that poor boy's death."

"Now, how did you know that?" I questioned with a slight smile. There was very little that happened in Key West that she didn't know about.

So, I continued, "You wouldn't mind talking to me about Brian, would you?"

"Darling, that assumption may not be accurate," she quipped.

"And why not?

"What do you want to know?"

"I want to find out who killed him."

"I know that's what you want, honey."

"Why not talk to me."

"I didn't say I wasn't.

"But I thought--"

"You didn't ask."

I stood there with a stupid grin across my face knowing I just lost that little duel.

"Ah. Right. Can I talk to you about Brian?"

"May I!"

"What?"

"The proper way to say it is, 'May I talk to you about Brian?' Didn't you take English in school?" She spoke to me like a mother to a little child.

All I could do was just stand there with that same stupid grin still hung on my face.

"You're a writer, honey. You're supposed to know how to say things proper like."

"Uh, may I talk to you?"

"Of course you can," she spoke with a twinkle in her eye and a kindness I hadn't heard in anyone since my mother died. "Here. Have a seat next to Miss Ruthie."

I pulled up a chair and sat. As I did, several members of the band walked out into the bar area.

Harvey spoke for the rest when he said, "Miss Ruthie, we're breaking for lunch a little early."

"That'll be fine. Y'all have fun, okay?

Harvey walked out onto the sidewalk, took out a cigarette and lit it. He took a few steps then stopped. The other members of the band walked on down Duval.

Ruthie leaned over to me, indicated Harvey with a nod and said, "Good drummer; sorry ass human."

"Oh?" I replied and paused as Ruthie poured a glass of ice water and handed it to me. "I don't know Harvey at all. So, what can you tell me about Brian?"

"Well, first, I need to know just why you're looking into Brian's death. That might help me to know what to tell you."

"That sounds reasonable. I'm going to write a tribute to Brian and about his career, you know, for the newspaper."

"Now that's a mighty fine purpose to be snooping around. I mean, that's the kind of thing you do."

"So what can you tell me?"

"What do you want to know, sweetie?"

"Whatever you can tell me."

"You're not very good at this, are you?"

"Compared to you? I guess not," I said with a reluctance that admitted my total lack of questioning ability. "I mean, I'm a writer, not an investigator."

I considered myself a pretty good researcher, especially when it was just me and a room with shelves of books, journals and old manuscripts. I could spend hours and find just what I needed. But, the ability to form and ask questions to illicit specific answers had always eluded me. This short-coming hindered me as a reporter but had aided me many times as a novelist.

Ruthie said, "All I know is he wasn't gay."

"Was that important?"

"Around here, sweetie? All the guys are gay as three dollar bills."

Feeling like I almost had the hang of it, I replied with, "Did that cause him any problems?"

"Well, about a week before he died, I overheard him arguing with someone in the dressing room. I knocked and asked if he was alright. He assured me he was fine."

"Do you know who it was, you know, that he was arguing with?"

"No. But, there was a lot of noise and the door was closed."

At this point, most of the members of the band had wandered off downtown. Styles stayed at the bar and ordered a ham sandwich and a beer.

"What were they arguing about?"

Ruthie paused a moment in thought. "I got the impression it was about sex. But then all the guys around here talk about sex most of the time — well, except when they're talking about music."

"The other voice was male?"

"Oh, yes. Definitely male. And loud."

"Okay. Thanks for your help."

"You get what you wanted?"

"Actually, I'm not sure, but I think what you've told me is important."

"Jay, honey?"

I had already stood and turned toward the sidewalk. So I paused and turned back to her. "Yes?"

"You be careful. Okay?"

"I will, Ruth."

I walked out onto the sidewalk and headed south on Duval Street. As I walked, I got a feeling that someone was following me, although I couldn't help but wonder why someone would want to do that. I mean, I'm no threat to anyone.

I'm just a writer who's working on a tribute to Brian, I considered. But after several more blocks of walking the feeling did not go away.

I looked behind me several times then ducked into an ally. People passed by. I stepped out and walked back the way I came. I stopped just before another alley, paused for a couple of moments then stepped into that alley and found myself face to face with Theo.

"Theo! What are you doing following me?"

"I'm sorry, Jay. But Perry was worried about you."

"That's nice, but--"

"So, he wanted me to keep an eye on you."

I couldn't help but chuckle when I looked at Theo and said, "Well, since you're here, I may as well ask you a couple of questions about Perry."

Theo's countenance dropped as his forehead creased

downward and his eyebrows pressed together. "I don't think I should."

"Perry said for me to investigate."

"Of course," he said, seemingly dropping his guard.

"Okay?"

"Sure. Go ahead."

"When did Perry first meet Brian?"

"I'm not sure. But, I think it was at the annual Gay Community Talent Show several years ago. Actually, I think it was five. Brian was performing his act as Britney."

"What precipitated the meeting?"

"I think it was because Perry was impressed with Brian's talent. He approached him and introduced himself."

"Did they talk any?"

"No, I don't think so. I just don't remember that much. They might have. I was busy talking to other people."

"What about the chief? Was she at that show?"

"I don't remember. No, wait. She's only been chief for a few months. She couldn't have been there."

"Do you remember the chief ever meeting and talking to Brian?"

"I remember that she was at Brian's performance at Ruth's a couple of months ago."

"Did she say anything to Brian or indicate that she knew him?"

"Not as I could tell. What's this all about?"

"I'm really not sure. How well did you know Brian?"

"He would come over to the house three or four times a year. We would visit and then he and Perry would spend time talking while I washed the dishes."

"He did. To Perry?"

"Yeah. We laughed a lot and talked a lot about stuff."

"What stuff?"

Theodore gave away a slight smile as he remembered. "He told us about his family and about this girl he knew."

"He told you both about that?"

"Yeah. He was so cute whenever he talked about her. You know I think he loved her, you know."

"Odd that Perry didn't mention you both knew all about Brian's past."

"You didn't ask," Theo said with an amusing smile.

"Well, that explains how it is that Perry knew so much about the girlfriend."

"I wouldn't say he knew all about her. I know Perry never met her."

"Well, I appreciate you telling me these things. Tell Perry that I'll be over in a couple of hours to report on what I've found out so far today."

"Oh, I almost forgot," Theo said. "Perry wants you to come over for dinner. I'm fixing Shrimp Creole. It's my specialty."

"Are you from Louisiana?"

"A long time ago, in another life. Grew up near Lafayette. Pure blooded Cajun French, mon ami. See you tonight."

"I'm looking forward to it. What time?"

"About seven-ish?"

"Great. See you then."

After we shook hands, Theo turned and walked in the direction of Perry's place; and I walked across Duval toward my own apartment. As I walked, the feeling that someone was following me continued to nag at me.

As I rounded the corner onto Eaton Street, I stopped and turned around looking back down Duval in hopes of catching the person following me. But the people who were walking along were normal tourists or locals I knew. No one seemed the slightest bit interested in me or even tried to avoid my eyes.

My mind raced. This criminal investigation is getting to me, I thought as I shook my head shaking off the feeling. Just then I heard a voice.

"Excuse me, sir, could you help us?"

I turned and looked into the strong eyes of a man who stood almost three inches above me. The man's smile and charm almost exploded off his face in radiance similar to the rays of the sun peaking above the horizon at sunrise.

I smiled and said, "Sure. What can I do for you?"

"This is my family," the man said as he pointed to a lady in her late thirties with well-manicured hair and clothing, a boy who seemed to be about fifteen, and a pre-teen girl dressed in a well cut sundress.

"We were wondering if you could direct us to the Hemingway House."

I stood there mesmerized for a moment, smiled, and said, "The best way to get there is to walk back down Duval to Truman, turn right, walk about two blocks, and turn right again on Whitehead. The house will be on your right."

"This is a lovely town, you have here, sir."

"Thank you. We're proud of it. I take it you're from out of town?"

"Yes, we're from Silverthorne, Colorado."

"No kidding?" I smiled with some enthusiasm. "My roommate at Emerson College lived in Silverthorne for a short time after we graduated. He moved to downtown Denver to work at the NBC affiliate there."

"Nine-News. The Big KUSA it is."

"Yes. He was hired to work as a producer; behind the scenes sort of guy, you know. He writes a lot of the stuff the other folks read."

The man smiled and replied with the obvious reply, "It's a small world, isn't it?"

I felt I was taking too much of their time and said a simple, "I hope you all have a wonderful vacation here in Key West. Oh, and a safe trip home."

We shook hands and the family turned and walked down Duval toward Truman. I just stood for a moment watching the nice family walk away as I smiled and thought, now there's the real Americana in action. I took a deep breath and walked down Eaton Street to my apartment.

As I approached my place, I remembered that I needed to run an errand. So, I turned and walked toward the side of the porch. I unlocked the little green and yellow scooter that I bought in order to ride around the island, started it up, and moved out onto Eaton where I turned and traveled down Whitehead to Southard.

‡   ‡   ‡

AT THE END OF SOUTHARD STREET, The Christian Center had set up a circus-type tent for their revival meetings in the center of a large hundred-acre vacant field. On the side of the tent a large tractor trailer type motor home was parked against the side where the podium stood. This was done so that the Reverend Santos could walk out of his palatial dressing room and onto the stage area without being disturbed by anyone or by well-wishers seeking autographs.

When I drove up to the tent, a security guard held up his hand to stop me near the front entrance. As I put on the brakes, the guard said, "I'm sorry, sir. The services won't start until seven o'clock this evening. You can come back then."

I smiled, got off the scooter, and said, "I'm here to see Reverend Champion."

The guard raised his voice a bit and insisted, "He's not available at this moment."

"Tell him that I'm here about Brian Silver."

"I said he's not available," the guard replied with sternness, putting his hand on his sidearm. "Now just move on along and stop bothering the pastors. They have too much to do before the services tonight."

Still not moving, I continued, "Well you tell him that I need to talk to him about Brian Silver's murder."

"Look, mister," the guard insisted again. "Just leave. Now. Come back tonight."

"I'm not going anywhere."

Just then, Marcus appeared from inside the tent. He walked over to where we were standing, placed his hand on the guard's shoulder and said in a calm and soothing voice,

"It's okay, Charles."

"Yes, sir," the guard replied and walked away, but not very far as if ready to jump to the pastor's aid.

Marcus turned, smiled at me and said, "He was just following orders. I'm Marcus Champion."

I gave a slight smile and said, "I'm Jay Morrison. I'm a writer."

"I'm sorry, Mr. Morrison," replied Marcus. "But we're not giving interviews for the papers at this point; but if you'll give me your card, we'll contact you with a press release later this afternoon."

"You misunderstand me, Reverend Champion. I'm not a reporter, I'm an author. The reason I'm here is because I have a lot of friends in the gay community, including Brian Silver, and I'm concerned about your presence here."

"You're a writer? Or are you actually a policeman?" questioned Marcus.

"I'm not a policeman, I'm just a writer; but I considered Brian a friend. He's helped me on some of my projects."

"What could I possibly tell you?"

"I understand that Brian visited you a day or so before he was shot."

"I think that's correct. I mean, I do not listen to the news very often so I'm not sure what date he died. But I guess that since you asked the question, you must already know the answer."

Caught a little off guard by Marcus's charming way of putting things, I pulled out my notepad and a pen.

"Would you mind telling me what the conversation was about?"

"Yes I do," he replied with a smile.

Marcus was not just charming he was also smart and quick on his feet. I stared at him for a moment.

Marcus continued. "But, I'll tell you it had nothing to do with his death."

"Maybe the police should decide that."

"You asked if I 'mind' telling you, which I do. I did not say I would 'not' tell you anything at all."

"Sorry about that."

"Now just what was it that you wanted to know?"

"I was asking why Brian came here before he died?"

"Brian was a member of our congregation before he moved to Key West and started hanging around with the perverts of this city. I was deeply saddened over his lapse into debauchery before his death."

"Why did he leave your church?"

"I believe it had something to do with another member. There were certain allegations that later proved not to be true. I guess he was just too embarrassed to stay. To be honest, I was not privy to any of what led to his leaving. I'm just telling you what I heard from other people who may or may not know what really happened."

"What was the nature of the charges?"

"Charges?"

"Yes. You said there were certain allegations. I just assumed that you were speaking of charges against him."

"Really, is it necessary to talk about all that?" Marcus said with a humble sounding concern for the privacy of one of his parishioners.

"Yes," I insisted again.

"A young boy accused him of homoerotic activities. The boy later recanted and said he was just mad at Brian because he wouldn't teach him how to play the piano the way he played. All the kids at the church admired Brian's musical talents, and many of them wanted him to teach them. Of course there was no way he could teach all of them. He had to turn this kid down. So the boy tried to hurt him."

"And so you think he moved to Key West to prove the boy wrong? Somehow that doesn't seem to make sense."

"I don't know anything about that. But I'll tell you this, a lot of people believed the boy."

"And what about Maria?"

"Who?"

"Maria Hernandez. I understand that she belongs to your church. You should know her."

"I don't know everybody who claims to be a member of the church. We have over twenty-five thousand people who attend on a regular basis. I don't recall her."

I paused and stared at Marcus for a few moments then said, "I guess that's all I have. I appreciate your taking time for me."

Marcus's face lit up with delight as he said, "I hope I've helped you in your pursuits. By the way, have you been to one of our revival services?"

"No."

"Oh?"

"And this conversation is not about me," Jay said.

"Well, you're welcome to attend anytime. I'll personally see that you get a good seat. We can talk again."

"I may not attend, but I can assure you that we'll be

talking again in the very near future."

I turned and walked back to my scooter as Marcus walked back into the tent. Just then, the guard stepped out from behind a truck and stopped me.

Frightened, I raised my arms, noticing that the guard was not making any aggressive movements. He was standing there with a just the slip of a smile.

He spoke quietly, "Mister, did I overhear that you are investigating Brain Silver's death?"

"Yes," I answered, looking back at the tent.

"I can't say for a fact, but scuttlebutt has it that Brian was Pastor John's son from Cuba."

"Are you sure about that? I mean, do you have any proof?"

"I'm just giving you a little gossip. Some people are saying his death was connected in some way to his relationship to Pastor Santos and that Brian was murdered, you know, to keep him quiet. What you do with this information is up to you."

I looked back toward the tent again just for a moment realizing I was learning nothing new. I turned back and I said, "I appreciate that. But--" The guard was no longer standing near me; he was nowhere to be seen.

I looked around for several more minutes hoping to see him. Finally, I shrugged, started up the scooter, and drove off toward Duval Street.

I saw that Marcus stood at the window of the motor home and watched us as we talked. Later I found out that when I drove off, he and Santos had a conversation that went something like this:

Marcus turned and said, "He was talking to the security guard."

"That's the least of our worries."

"What do you mean?"

"We've got to do something about this Brian thing. It might be a real problem for us here."

"I didn't figure on Brian's possible impact on our ministry. I guess I didn't know just how popular he had become after he left Miami."

"I gave that gentleman the line about a boy. I think he bought it. Is there anything else? Do you want me to take care of him?"

"No, Marcus. I think this time I'll take care of this myself."

As for me, I felt sure that I was on the right track for a story and to help Perry with the case. So as I drove back to my place, I had a big smile on my face.

Fourteen

Thursday Evening, November Fifth

PERRY WAS SITTING in his favorite chair on the patio, his pain showing in the creases around his face, trying valiantly not to show it. Theodore and I were both seated near him at TV trays. When we finished the meal, Theodore stood and picked up the dishes from each tray and took them into the kitchen.

I scratched my stomach, loosened my belt, looked at Theo just before he went into the kitchen, and said, "My God, Theo, I haven't eaten that much in years. That was the most delicious meal I've ever had."

"I'm glad you liked it, Jay," he said as he glanced back to me before walking through the opened sliding glass doors to the main part of the house.

I looked over at Perry.

"Do you eat this way every night?"

"Good God, no! Otherwise I'd be three hundred pounds by now. No, he cooks like this on the few occasions we have company."

I smiled.

There was a long pause as Theo came into the room carrying a tray with several cups of coffee, cream, and sugar. He stopped in front of me as I helped myself to a cup and a spoon of sugar. He turned to Perry who took both cream and sugar, stirred his coffee, and placed the spoon back on the try. Theo walked back into the kitchen and shut the door.

"So, what's his story?"

"His story? Theo was born to a highly respected and wealthy landowner in Thibodaux, Louisiana. I think his great-grandfather was one of the city fathers. He donated part of the land on which Nichols State University sits. As the eldest son of one of the wealthiest families in the area, Theodore was supposed to take on the mantle of prestige the family had known for five generations."

"Where did they get their wealth?"

"They sold the oil rights on their vast holdings after black gold was discovered in the swamps surrounding their land."

"And he's so unassuming. You'd never know he was rich."

"I know. Theodore graduated from Louisiana State University with a degree in history and was accepted into the law school. He told me once that he used to sit on the balcony of the student center and look over at the law school building. He longed for the day he would be studying there."

"Theo's a lawyer?"

"Actually, no. Let me explain. After his graduation, his father took him to New Orleans to celebrate his twenty-first birthday. This was going to be his rite of passage. His father got him drunk on Bourbon Street then put him in the hands of a good looking whore at his favorite house on Royal Street."

"Money does have it privileges."

"When Theodore had trouble performing, the lady laughed at him and called him a girlie boy. He didn't get mad. He just stood up, put his clothes back on, and walked out of the house."

"Wow. What happened next?"

"He walked twenty blocks or so to the Greyhound bus station and bought a ticket for Jacksonville, Florida. He sat down on one of the benches to wait for his bus to arrive. At around two-thirty in the morning, the bus pulled into the station and the boarding call sounded for east bound passengers. Theo stood, boarded the bus, and rode out of New Orleans and out of his family's life."

"I can't imagine what that must have been like."

"In a way, I think I know exactly what he felt. After arriving in Jacksonville, he started walking south on U.S. Highway One hoping to catch a ride with someone. He left so quickly that he had little cash and no credit cards on him. It took him three days to walk and hitch hike until he was standing on the corner of Duval Street and Truman Avenue in Key West wondering just what he would do next."

"Where did he learn to develop so much patience?"

"I've often wondered that myself. I suppose it comes to him naturally."

"Then what happened?"

"So, after arriving, he walked north on Duval until he noticed a small bulletin board. A small note that I had posted caught his eye. On it was the following message typed out neatly; 'needed: housekeeper who can also type and do office work.'"

"So that's how you two hooked up?"

"At the bottom of the note I had placed several small pieces torn with a phone number on each. Theo pulled off one and called me from a nearby pay phone. When the conversation ended, I invited him to my place where we talked for two hours. I offered him the job. When I asked for an address and phone number he admitted he had just arrived that morning and had no place to stay."

"Oh, man. I'm all ears."

"I took him to the guest bedroom and asked if that room would meet his needs. Theo looked at it, smiled, dropped his backpack on the bed and never left."

"I see." At this point, I looked around toward the kitchen and asked, "Uh, Isn't he going to join us for coffee?"

"He knows we need to talk about the case and doesn't want to hear about it. He's learned that the less he knows about what I do, the better off he feels. So, what have you found out?"

"I'm not sure if what I have is worth anything."

"I'll be the judge of that. Just tell me everything you've heard up until now."

"Okay. Some of this is just speculation, but I've had several people tell me some of the same things." I paused for a moment and took a couple of sips of coffee.

Apparently impatient, Perry said, "Go ahead."

"It seems that the girlfriend had some kind of problem with The Christian Center, and I don't think it was just about membership or theology. Something big must have happened causing Brian to leave town, and I'm thinking it must have had something to do with her and Brain."

Perry pondered that for a moment then said, "Brian once told me that he had a big fight with someone in Miami about a girl. I figured it must have been a street fight or something; but now I'm wondering if it had something to do with the church and the pastor."

"I wonder why?"

"I thought it might have to do with Brian's past or something like that; but now with what we've discovered, I can't help but think there must have been something more at stake, something more than just Brian's past or his present."

"Perhaps he didn't want the fact to come out that Brian was his illegitimate son."

"You may have something there. The chief is checking that aspect as we speak."

"It sure gives the right-reverend a good motive for keeping Brian quiet. His boy could have ruined his conservative Christian reputation in Miami."

"But, murder?" Perry said as he shook his head.

"Unless Brian was in a position to ruin his revival in Key West."

"Wait," Perry said as he paused for a long moment. I

could see the pain on his face as he seemed to hide it. He continued. "That would have cost him a lot of money."

"I'm no mystery writer, but I've seen a lot of police dramas on television. Hasn't money, lots of money, always been a good motive for murder?"

"I'll need to talk to the chief about this to see just what she's turned up." Perry smiled, amused at my comment.

Perry took another sip from his coffee cup then continued pausing the conversation.

"Jay, you may have just put your finger on something really important."

"I hope I've been of some help."

"We'll find out soon," Perry said. "I hope."

"It's getting late." I yawned as I stood and said, "I need to hit the hay."

"You didn't get any of Theodore's famous Key Lime pie."

Theodore came in with a tray and three plates each with a big piece of Key Lime pie on them.

"I'm sorry, Theo. I couldn't possibly get it down after that magnificent dinner. I mean the creole? It was wonderful!"

Theo put down the tray and said, "Thank you, Jay."

He handed me a bag folded in a neat crease across the top.

"And you might want this for tomorrow. It's a piece of my Key Lime Pie to go."

I smiled big and took the bag. "You're just too much, my friend."

Perry reached out his hand as I stood and walked over

to his chair. I shook hands with a gentle, yet firm hold.

"Take care of yourself," Perry said.

I walked to the front door. Theodore followed and opened the door for me. I had not yet walked through the door when I dropped my keys. So, I bent over to pick them up and hit them with my foot. I leaned down further as I reached for the keys back inside the house.

As Theodore stood waiting to close the door, there was a strong thud against the door then the sound of a gunshot rang out. The door pushed Theo back into the room causing him to fall on the floor.

I dove back toward the wall as Theodore yelled out, "What the hell?"

I crawled on the floor, grabbed the bottom of the door and slammed it shut.

Perry yelled out, "My God! Theo, are you alright?"

Theo crawled with swift movements part of the way then ran over to where Perry was seated, knelt on the floor, and said, "I think I'm fine. What about you?"

"I'm okay. Jay? Where are you? Are you okay?"

I lifted myself up with care and looked out onto the patio at Theo and Perry who were hugging each other.

"I think I'm okay," I spoke out, "but, it sounded like somebody just tried to kill me!"

"You think?" Perry extended in dulcet tones.

"I believe we've made somebody mad."

Trembling, I crawled to the front window and looked out through a small slit between the blinds and the wall. I scanned the front yard and down Charles to Duval Street. After a minute or so I turned back to the inside and tried to speak. But my voice sounded more like a little mouse than me, "Somebody's upset about something. That bullet missed me by inches. I mean I heard it go by my ear."

That's when I dropped down onto the couch.

Perry stood with a cane and walked into the house from the patio and over to the sofa leaving Theo shaking on the floor next to the wheel chair. He looked at me and said, "You'd better be glad that he was a bad shot."

"What makes you think it's a he?"

Perry shrugged his shoulders as he said, "Just a figure of speech. But who's complaining?"

"Not me," I admitted as I mopped my brow with a couple of tissues.

While we talked, Theo walked back into the front room, looked out the window, and said, "I think whoever it was has gone. At least I don't see any movement out there."

I walked over to the door and opened it slightly to look out down the alley.

"Well. Perry," I sighed, "I think you'd better call your friends down at the police station."

Theodore had the phone in his hand and had already started speaking. "We've had a shooting at Perry Savant's house. Please send someone right away."

‡　　　‡　　　‡

AN HOUR LATER, Charles Street bustled with police activity. Crime scene tape was strewn from the intersection of Duval all the way down to Perry's house blocking off all traffic from Telegraph Lane. Fatima and Detective Hernandez stood with me getting my statement. Another officer was talking with Theodore and writing down everything he said.

Five uniformed officers accompanied the crime scene investigation team to help secure the area. One stood guard at the intersection of Charles and Duval. Two others stood at each end of Telegraph Lane blocking all traffic. The other two officers were assisting the detectives combing the street and grassy areas for possible clues to what happened.

Two members of the crime scene unit had set up their large briefcases and were processing every piece of evidence that was picked up. Two others went around to the other side of the house to see if they could find any signs of activity there.

I worked at being calm, but my hands shook when I held them out. As I looked down at them, I remembered the night I was called to go to investigate and report on a pile-up on the freeway. Approaching the scene, I felt ill at my stomach, not just emotionally repulsed. I got out of the car and walked over to where a semi had hit an auto ahead of it so hard that it slid up on top of the other, crushing the car below.

I looked at an arm that hung out of the lower car's window bent in a direction other than it was made to bend. Blood was everywhere in and outside of both vehicles. I stood stunned for a long time until I felt something happening inside my own belly. I ran from the road to some nearby bushes.

With my heart still racing, I shook back to reality as I realized that Fatima had just asked me a question. "I'm not sure what happened exactly," I said. "All I know is that I heard a bullet whiz past my ear almost as if it missed me by an inch or two. I could not only hear it, but I could swear that I felt the breeze."

"That's understandable," Fatima replied. "The shooter may have been near the end of the alley about where that uniformed officer is standing. And from the looks of the slug in the door, he was using a twenty-two revolver; terribly inaccurate at that distance, especially in the hands of an amateur. And that would also explain why we did not find a spent cartridge anywhere along Charles Street."

"The same caliber weapon as Brian Silver's murderer used," Hernandez said speaking like an after-thought.

Fatima nodded in agreement.

"You'd think with all the people on Duval Street that someone would have seen something," I interjected.

"They probably did but don't want to get involved. That's typical around here. And with something going on that late at night. I would venture a guess that they didn't know what they were seeing or hearing because they were too drunk to care or notice."

As I stood looking around, my mind once again went back to the scene at the accident as a cub reporter. I remembered that after going to the bushes and getting the revulsion out of my system, I went back to the scene and completed my assignment. Anyone who knew me very well understood that nothing gets in the way of Jay Morrison and a good story.

I sighed trying to calm myself down. "A real shame since the same thing happened with Brian."

"Just like at the murder scene," Theodore pointed out.

"What's that you said?" another detective inquired.

Theodore added, "You know, all those people on Duval Street less than ten feet from Brian when he was shot and no one saw a single thing. And that just makes me so mad. I mean, people are so selfish and self-centered, they don't ever think that maybe they could help someone else. Instead they 'don't want to get involved' and go about their merry way. When it happens to them, they get pissed off and bitch about the people who never seem to stop to help out. It's just a crying shame."

Fatima, Hernandez and I all stood in awe of this big quiet guy. Seldom have any of us heard that many words come out of his mouth at any one time.

I interjected, "Uh, yeah. Well, one thing is for sure. Someone's upset about our investigation."

"I wonder if Brian's murderer is afraid we're getting too close. Or at least someone's afraid we might suspect him, or her," Fatima added.

"What if the target was not Jay?" Hernandez said.

"What?" I shot back.

"You've got a point there," Fatima offered. "I couldn't help but wonder the same thing when I arrived. I mean, how did the shooter know you were even in the house, Jay, unless he had followed you here, stood over there all evening waiting for you to come out? I find that risky at best and not very smart at worst. No, he came just before you left for a reason."

Theo's face scrunched up as if in deep thought as he said, "You know, it was about a quarter to ten when Jay was leaving. I usually take Perry out for his walk every night between nine-thirty and quarter 'til. I mean, we're like clockwork on our walks."

"The shooter knew your schedule and was waiting for the two of you to come through the door," Hernandez added, looking at Theo.

"Looking at where the bullet struck the door," Fatima said. "He could have been aiming at someone in a wheelchair rather than someone walking."

"Jay, you walked out at the wrong time," Hernandez pointed out.

"At least I ducked at the right time," I insisted.

"What?" the detective pleaded.

"I dropped my car keys and bent over to pick them up."

"The shooter must have turned to look at the moment you bent down and thought you were in a wheelchair," Hernandez interjected.

"Oh, my god, I didn't turn on the light. It was dark at the door. What luck," Theodore added.

"I'd say so. Look, I'm gonna get back to my apartment. I don't think I'll ever get to sleep tonight."

"Okay," Fatima said. "But just in case, I want one of these officers to escort you home. I'll station another to stay here and keep an eye on Theo and Perry for the night."

"You're not taking any chances, are you?"

"Absolutely!" Fatima stated. "Not with murder."

"Thanks," I stated as I shook her hand and the detective's hand. I shook Theo's hand and said, "Theo, the creole was terrific. Thanks for everything."

Theo turned to Fatima and said, "I'm going in now."

"We'll finish up out here. This officer will hang around until morning."

"Thank you," Theo replied.

I turned to the officer next to me and said, "I'm going in with Theo to say good night to Perry."

He nodded agreement; and I went in.

The other officers helped the Crime Scene Investigative Assistant take up the yellow tape. When they finished, they all left as one officer stayed next to the door for the evening.

Inside the house, Theo and I walked over to Perry who had dozed off in the chair. He reached down and touched his cheek as a mother would a small child.

As Theo stroked the pale and sunken cheek of the man he had grown so fond of, Perry opened his eyes and looked at his friend. Then this rough-edged street cop from the mean streets of New York City spoke in a tone so foreign even he didn't recognize it.

"I was so scared. I just knew something had happened to you. I couldn't stand the thought of that ever."

"I know, my love," Theo replied as a single tear rolled down his cheek. "Jay wanted to tell you 'good-bye' before he left. Plus, it's time to go to bed."

Perry lifted his eyes toward me and stretched out his arm.

I took his hand and said, "Perry, please rest well. We've got a lot to accomplish over the next several days."

"I will."

Theo reached over and gently picked up Perry into his arms and carried him to the bedroom. As he reached the door, he leaned over and with his pinky finger caught the light switch and the lights in the living area fell into darkness. He walked into the bedroom where a sliver of light from the street lamp outside offered just enough illumination to allow Theo to navigate to the bed.

He gently laid Perry down, turned on the lamp next to the bed, and helped him into his pajamas. He went into the bathroom, got a glass of water, and gently placed toothpaste on a toothbrush. He brought the items to Perry who bushed his teeth without much energy.

As he finished, Theo took the items back into the bathroom, rinsed them off and carefully placed them back to their original positions in the cabinet. He brushed his own teeth, washed his face, and returned to where Perry was lying.

Almost as if participating in a religious ritual, he helped Perry under the covers, tucking him in with a careful and gentle tug. He stood up and looked down at the once virile body he had come to know as a caring smile crossed his lips. He leaned down and lightly kissed his dear friend on the forehead.

Perry reached up and placed his hand on Theo's cheek and said, "What did I ever do to deserve you?"

"Hush," Theo whispered. "Rest."

Then this gentle giant of a man reached over and turned off the light by the bed and lay down next to this man who had become more than a surrogate father but a mentor and lover. He held him close with great tenderness as he gently waited to hear the soft, even, snoring of Perry's deep sleep.

He lay there looking at his lover with a deep knowledge that their time together was coming to a close too soon. A tear slowly rolled down Theo's cheek and gently dropped to his forearm. Theo did not move.

I quietly picked up the bag with the pie I had dropped, slipped out the door. The officer joined me as we walked back to my place. I had to wonder just what I had done in my life to deserve such friends as Theo and Perry.

Fifteen

Friday, November Sixth

I FINALLY FELL ASLEEP on the couch sometime around four, but found myself wide awake before the sun began creeping above the horizon. Hungry and tired from the previous night's activities, I left the house noticing that the police officer was still standing near my house. I shook his hand.

"Thank you for your diligence in protecting me."

"I reported no activities overnight. So, I was told to ask if you need me to stay."

"I don't think that's necessary. But, I'll treat you to breakfast if you want to come with me."

"I appreciate that, Mr. Morrison. But, I should get back to the station and write up my report so I can get home."

I thanked him, hopped on the scooter, rode to the Monument Street Café, parked on the sidewalk, and walked in for breakfast. After being seated, I ordered my regular meal and coffee. I pulled out my computer and started to type on my latest project.

Although the Brian Silver murder had taken a lot of my time over the past few days, I was keenly aware that the deadline set by my publisher hung heavy over me. The book I was writing had to be finished.

Although I was not really happy with how the ending of the story was developing, I decided to just go with the expected rather than trying to contrive some sort of surprise ending for a rather routine novel about love, greed, and revenge.

I thought about it for a while but decided to just let the hero and the villain kill each other. I looked down and started pounding at the keys.

Around eleven I started to pack up when Maria walked up to me and said, "I was told you'd be here."

Startled, I stood with a great big smile on my face, and said, "Maria. What a surprise. Uh, have a seat. I'm really happy to see you!"

"Thank you."

"What brings you to Key West?"

Maria sighed, sat across from me, and said, "I've been worried."

"About what?"

"Things are going on at the church, you know? There's all kinds of gossip about the pastor. People are saying some awful things. There are even people talking as if something's going on in Key West."

"What are they saying?"

As the waitress walked up to the table, Maria looked at her and said, "Get me a cup of vegetable soup and a grilled chicken sandwich. Oh, and a Diet Coke."

After the waitress left, Maria looked at me, her eyebrows furled, and said, "The talk is that he's done something bad this time; really bad."

"What? What kind of things are they saying he did?"

"That's just it. No one is saying. Or no one's really sure. But it sounds big. And you know, maybe that's why he's pushing this Key West crusade so much."

"How so?"

"Well, he's got to do something major in order to take the focus away from anything else he's done. I mean, there is so much talk and yet nothing solid or of any substance. Do you have any idea what's going on? I mean what have you found out down here?"

"Actually, I haven't discovered much at all, which is frustrating. I wish, I mean, I'm so frustrated about this whole thing."

"Do you think it's something else?"

I paused for a moment to take a last swig of coffee.

"I have my suspicions as to what might be going on, but I have nothing definite."

"Tell me," Maria pressed.

"I can't. But if I'm correct, the whole Christian Center Empire is going to crumble."

"Wow," Maria whispered under her breath.

The waitress brought the soup, sandwich and coke and

set them down in front of Maria and asked, "Do you need anything else?" to which we both shook our heads.

Waiting for the waitress to leave, I turned to Maria and said, "So what else do you need to tell me? There is more, isn't there?"

"I just thought this stuff was important. And I wanted to be here to see things when they happen. You know. When the murderer is found?" She picked up her sandwich and began to eat, stopping every so often to have some soup.

I spoke, "I don't think the police are ready to make an arrest anytime soon."

"But with what I just told you?"

"I don't know what that means, but I'll pass that onto the detectives in charge of the investigation."

"You don't believe it's--"

I looked straight at her, took a deep breath, and said, "Personally, I'm not yet convinced that Brian was killed by anyone at the church."

Maria thought about that and whistled under her breath. "Really? Why?"

"I think the motive is all wrong. Maybe Santos might try to ruin Brian or smear his name in Miami in order to protect his own reputation, but murder? I don't see it. At least I can't see anything positive coming out of Brian's murder as it concerns The Christian Center itself, or even Pastor Santos."

"Who do you think did it?"

"I don't have a clue," I had to admit. "The bottom line is just that I'm not convinced it's the reverend."

"What about his assistant?" she wondered.

"Marcus? He seems capable of murder in my opinion,

but right now I can't see why he would. That's a bit much to protect someone else's reputation. Champion would gladly throw himself on a grenade to protect Santos, but murder? I would be surprised if that turns out to be the case."

"Well, I'm sorry I wasted your time," Maria said with a sort of disappointment in her voice.

"You didn't waste my time," I reassured her. "What you've done is convince me I'm correct."

"How?"

"If Marcus killed Brian, the church people wouldn't be just talking about it, they'd be up in arms and crying for Santos' head on a platter for allowing that. No, the gossip you've been hearing is related to something else. Either it has to do with the talk that Brian was Santos' son from his life in Cuba, or it's all about something we're not aware of at this point."

She finished her sandwich and soup then drank down the rest of her Coke.

"I'll be here for the next week or so helping out at the tent revival. I'm spending part of my vacation time as a volunteer so if there's anything I can do to help you find Brian's killer--"

"Actually there is."

"Oh, wow! What do you want me to do?" Maria asked with wide-eyed enthusiasm.

"I'd like for you to go with me to see Perry later today. In the meantime, where are you staying?"

"I'm staying with a girlfriend from high school. She runs a youth hostel called the Caroline House down here in old town somewhere."

I know right where that is. Can I run you over there?"

"No, that's not necessary. She's coming to the restaurant to pick me up in about twenty minutes."

"Good," Jay said. "I'll pick you up around seven this evening. Here's my cell phone number in case you need to call me." I took out a calling card and wrote a telephone number on the back and handed it to her.

"I'll see you then," she said as I picked up my things and walked out of the restaurant. I got on the scooter and rode off toward the tent revival location. It was a beautiful day. The sky was clear, the sun shone bright, and the air was warm.

I weaved along the street toward the park where the tent revival was being held. As I approached the tent, there were numerous people milling around. I pulled up, parked the scooter, entered the tent area, and walked to the front where several men and women were picking up the trash from the night before.

I stopped a man nearby and said, "Excuse me. Where can I find Marcus Champion?"

The man pointed over toward the very expensive looking motor home parked at the rear of the tent. It had been moved from where it was the night before and pulled more out of sight of the parking lot. I walked over to the trailer door and knocked.

A voice from inside said, "Come in!"

I opened the door and walked in. Marcus Champion and John Santos were seated at the table going over some paperwork. They both stood politely.

Marcus Champion spoke first, "Jay Morrison, right? I

thought I remembered that correctly. Please meet Pastor John Santos of the Christian Center in Miami."

With grace, I replied, "Honored, sir."

"The honor is mine," Santos replied, "I've read several of your books. Your history is well researched and authentic. I, for one, appreciate good writing as well as authentic research that delves beyond the simplicity of history books and brings to life the reality of years gone by."

"Well, thank you so much. I can use all the accolades I can get. And if you don't mind, perhaps you could mention my books some evening from the pulpit?"

"I'll consider that. You deserve all the accolades, my friend. Coffee?"

"Thank you. A little sugar." John poured the coffee and sat.

Marcus spoke first. "To what do we owe this honor?"

"As you may know, I'm looking into the death of Brian Silver."

"A tragic event," lamented Marcus.

"How can we help you?" the pastor encouraged.

"Pastor, I'd like to ask you a few questions about Brian's background."

"Have the police completed their investigation?"

"Not as far as I know, but since Brian was a friend of mine, I feel compelled to find out all I can because I am writing a tribute for the local paper."

"That's admirable."

"Brian had become a sort of institution in this town. In my opinion he was the best impersonator ever to perform here."

I stopped and took a sip of coffee finding myself whispering, "Whoa. This is good coffee." I put down the coffee cup and said, "I was just wondering what you can tell me about Brian?"

"Not a lot, I'm afraid. I knew him after he joined our congregation about ten years ago."

"Did you know his parents?"

"I think he was an immigrant, wasn't he?" replied Marcus without a sign of guilt or discomfort.

"I think he came here from Cuba," Santos volunteered.

"Isn't that where you're from, Pastor?"

John paused a moment then said, "Yes. But you already knew that."

"Did you know his parents over there?"

"Cuba is a large country."

Staring at Santos for a moment, I thought, this guy's as good as any politician I've ever met. So, I tried a little different strategy. "I thought perhaps you might have talked to Brian since he had immigrated like you did. The Cuban community is not that big in Miami."

At this point Marcus jumped in and said, "We both knew Brian as a very troubled member of our youth department when he first came to us. The Lord used the church members to help him with his problems. Way back then we thought that he had gotten out of that lifestyle."

"What lifestyle?" I asked.

Caught, Marcus mumbled, "You know-"

"No. I don't know."

"Listen, Mr. Morrison, we didn't know Brian well. We heard that he had changed his name when he came to the

U.S.; but neither of us knew who he was in Cuba. There was no way John or I could have known him before he arrived at our church."

"I understand."

At this point, Santos looked hard at Marcus and made a simple gesture with his eyebrow.

Marcus said, "So, is there anything else we can help you with?"

I paused a bit but said, "Probably not. I appreciate your time."

I started to leave then stopped at the door. I quickly turned back to the pastor and said, "Oh, I heard a rumor that you were Brian's father."

Without batting an eyelash, Santos replied, "I heard that rumor, too."

"And what do you say about it?"

At this point Marcus jumped in.

"There are a lot of people who would like to defame Pastor John. I wouldn't believe those rumors if I were you."

"Well, you're not me, are you?"

Marcus paused. "No."

There was another long, difficult pause. Santos interjected, "If we hear anything at all that we think you might be interested in, we'll be glad to call you, after we inform the police."

"Thank you," I said knowing I was being dismissed.

I walked out of the trailer, walked over to the scooter, and drove off. As I turned east out of the parking lot, I couldn't help but wonder just what was going on. It was obvious that the two men were definitely covering up something, but what I could not figure out.

‡   ‡   ‡

IT WAS NEARING six o'clock as I made my way across town and pulled up in front of The Caroline House. I parked the scooter on the sidewalk next to the porch and started up the stairs. Just then, Maria came bounding out of the door like a teenager ready to head out on some dramatic adventure or road trip.

Watching her jet black hair blowing in the breeze, I wondered if I had ever met anyone as interesting and exciting as she. There was a spirit about her that I had never seen or recognized in any other woman I had known. She stood before me almost like an angel draped in pink and white, her nicely tanned legs looking longer than ever. I couldn't help but admire and perhaps even desire her. Yet, I felt guilty about that. This was Brian's girl!

"Okay!" she almost shouted out. "Let's go meet the famous NYPD detective turned flamer."

I stood for a moment looking at her. She seemed to glow in the lowering western sun's light which cut through the trees bathing her in a sort of spotlight effect. That's when I realized that if I had only met someone like her ten years ago; but I knew such thoughts were counterproductive. Yet, I couldn't help myself.

At that I jerked back to the present with the thought, I need to keep my focus on the job at hand.

Yet, whenever I looked at her, I couldn't stop thinking

just how beautiful and full of life she was. I stood there staring and smiling.

"What?" she said.

"Oh, uh, nothing; let's go."

And I jumped onto the scooter and headed down the street toward Perry's place.

When we arrived at the back entrance, Maria's hand was only inches from the latch of the outer gate when Theo answered the door causing her to jump back. Theo looked puzzled at first then noticed me locking the scooter to a nearby pole.

He spoke with a smile in his voice. "You must be Maria. I'm Theo, Perry's partner and personal assistant."

Maria stuck out her hand and shook Theo's with a manly firmness that caught him a bit off guard.

"Nice grip," he whispered aloud.

"I believe in being strong first, then soft and feminine. What about you?"

Theo looked at her with an amused look and said, "Um, I guess ... well, come on in."

He stepped back as we walked into the back patio which always appeared well manicured with an old fashioned royal garden-like atmosphere. Perry was seated in a lounge chair. I walked over to him with Maria as Theo stepped into the house.

"Perry, I want you to meet Maria Hernandez."

"Ah, Brian's fiancé. I always knew that Brian had great taste. Now I'm convinced."

"You're very kind. Brian spoke of you many times."

"Lies," Perry interjected, "All lies."

Maria smiled and broke into a sort of shy laugh.

"Really? He thought you were a fair and kind man."

Perry reached out and took her hand, kissed it, and said to her, "Your beauty brightens up this dreary old atmosphere. So, you are very welcome in this place. Now, please sit down."

Maria and I sat in a couple of outdoor chairs nearby.

Before we could begin to talk about Brian and the incidents surrounding his death, Theo walked in with several TV trays and set them in front of each person then set one for himself. Theo then inquired as to what everyone wanted to drink. We each told him, after which he went back to the kitchen. Less than a minute later he was back outside with the drinks on a tray. He set the appropriate drink before each person.

He walked back into the kitchen and returned to the patio a couple of minutes later with a tray filled with dishes of shrimp étouffée piled high on the fluffiest white rice I had ever seen.

Perry said, "Please excuse the lack of small talk before dinner, but Theo is very punctual and believes in eating upon arrival at his home. He wants people fat and happy."

Maria and I laughed as Theo finished bringing in everything and setting the items before each of us. For the next several minutes we savored the elegant taste of Theo's recipe that almost melted in our mouths. Perry was the first to break the soft groans of pleasure that filled the patio.

"Theo, that was absolutely wonderful."

Maria remarked, "I've never tasted anything quite like this."

"It's actually my grandmother's recipe. Whenever I cook this, the aroma reminds me of how the smells from her kitchen would fill the house as everyone would get so excited about the meal to come."

We sat for several more minutes, enjoying dinner, as we washed down the shrimp with Theo's special cold-brewed iced tea. At last, Theo stood, picked up each person's empty plate and took them to the kitchen.

Before he could leave, I asked, "Perry, Maria's heard some things that seem to be going on at The Christian Center."

"Please, my dear, tell me about it."

She paused for a moment in deep thought.

Perry spoke gently, "Maria?"

She looked at him just as he noticed a grimace on her face. She said, "Now that I think about it, I'm not sure I know anything at all."

"Maria," Perry said with a caring look that betrayed the hard, NYPD detective exterior he tried his best to wear. "Tell me what you've heard. Let me decide whether or not it's important."

Maria delayed in an almost uncharacteristic way. Actually, from the moment we first met, I was impressed with her command of the situation, her self-confidence, her ability to figure out what was going on, and her decisiveness to act on her instincts. Yet, here on the back patio in Perry's presence, it looked like she was cowering like a small child almost afraid to speak.

Later I learned that Perry's appearance was like that of her own grandfather whom she totally adored. He had endured so much at the hands of the Castro regime in Cuba until he was able to escape with his family to the United States. In late 1999, he had helped her father to lead a small group of men in a plot to assassinate Fidel Castro at a major event in New York City that Fidel was scheduled to attend.

Unfortunately, the Cuban dictator fell ill the day before and did not show up. At about the same time, members of the Clinton administration discovered what the Cuban refugees were planning.

What happened after that is pure speculation since no one has ever been able to uncover any proof of the events that followed. The timing was interesting if not precise. On April 22, 2000, federal officials rolled into Miami and took Elian Gonzalez from his relatives in order to return him to Cuba.

That same evening, as Maria's father was leaving his business, a van pulled up and several men dressed in black with black hoods over their heads grabbed him and threw him into the van and drove off. Although there were several witnesses, no one was able to get the license number or what the men looked like. All they could say was that they believed Maria's father was kidnapped.

It seemed like a James Bond movie the way things happened. The sad part was that three days later, he was found in his own car underneath the Rickenbacker Causeway in about three feet of water. The coroner said he died of injuries from an automobile accident that caused his car to go over the side and land upside down below the pilings near the shoreline. Two years later, her grandfather died of an apparent heart attack.

Maria looked at Perry and seemed to melt into his deep, dark brown eyes thinking she was once again getting in touch with the grandfather she adored and the father she had lost. She took a deep breath and began as if she had just been caught by her daddy with her hand in the box of cookies high in the cabinet. With a light tear in her eye, she looked at him and spoke.

"People are talking about an investigation of some kind. And they're saying that the pastor may be in trouble. I think it's probably over the money in the church. I couldn't find out any specifics, but the rumors are flying from nearly everyone's lips that I know."

"Did it have to do with the revival here in the Keys?" Perry probed.

"Actually, the talk seems to center around the church in Miami and not the revival. The people I talked to have a lot of international connections and dealings. And they are the ones who had opposed the very thought of attempting to start a new church in Key West or anywhere else in the Keys. I think the problems might be related to all that, but I'm not really sure."

"Good," Perry said as if that solved the mystery.

"Good? Good?" I interjected. "What are you talking about? You know something?"

"Not really," Perry added, "I've been hearing some of the same things Maria's heard."

"About Brian?"

"Nothing solid," Perry continued, "but I wouldn't put it past Champion or Santos to have been involved in Brian's death in some way. And I wouldn't be surprised if Brian's death has something to do with all their international dealings."

"Do you want me to look into that angle?" I questioned.

"No. I said I wouldn't be surprised if they were involved in Brian's death; but at this point I'm still not convinced that they actually had anything to do with it. I need you to talk to the members of the band and see what they have to say. I think they know a lot more than they've been willing to tell the police. They might open up to you."

"Why are they important?"

"Just a hunch. Trust me. I'll do some looking into this other thing. I also need to update the chief."

Maria injected, "What can I do?"

"You can go with Jay and keep him out of trouble. Oh, wait a moment. Theo!" Theo entered.

"Yes, dear?"

"Get that pistol out of the top drawer of the desk.

"The pistol? Are you sure?"

"Yes. Please."

Theo paused a moment then spoke in a soft almost tortured voice as he said, "Okay."

He walked into the other room as I looked at Perry with a serious penetrating question, "What's that for?"

"I want you to take it. I'm afraid we may be getting too close and you may be in danger."

"I don't do guns."

"I don't care."

Theo re-entered with the pistol held by the handle with his thumb and forefinger as if he were holding a highly poisonous snake or a deadly creature. He handed the pistol to me. I would not take it. I only stared at it then looked over at Perry and admitted, "I hate guns."

"What about you, Maria?"

"Honestly, Perry. I wouldn't know what to do with it. I've never used a gun before and would rather not have them around me."

"Okay," Perry resigned, "Just be careful. Will you?"

"We will. And I promise to call you when I get something," I said.

Maria and I walked out the gate to the patio rather than walking through the house.

We rode in silence back to the hostel. When we arrived, Maria asked, "Jay, why did Perry offer to give us a pistol to carry with us?"

"I think he feared for our safety."

"Okay, but didn't he know you well enough that you would not take it?"

"I guess. I'm not sure."

"So, why did he offer it to me after offering it to you?"

"Maybe he wanted to see how you'd react."

"He was testing us, wasn't he?"

I sat on the scooter silent. I had no answer and did not want to speculate.

Maria continued, "Okay, here's another one for you. Did Theo seem as scared of that pistol to you as he did to me?"

"Oh, well, I can explain that. You see, Theo actually told me all about that one night at a dinner party Perry held for several of the leaders of the gay community."

"And you were there?" Maria said with an expression I was unsure how to interpret.

"Yes, I was invited. And no, I don't know why. Anyway, he related to me how after his twelfth birthday his father took him hunting in the woods near their home. He carried two rifles, a shotgun, and a pistol for them to use. They walked for several miles until his father signaled to freeze. He pointed up into the trees where Theo could see a squirrel sitting on a limb of a tree some fifteen feet or so above their heads. His father raised the shotgun and handed it to Theo indicating that he was to shoot at the small animal. Theo obeyed and pulled the trigger."

"He shot the poor little squirrel?"

"The squirrel was knocked off the branch and fell against the branch below and then to the ground. Still twitching, the squirrel lay there for several minutes pulling with his front legs as if trying to escape. The life left the tiny creature in front of Theo as he stood there looking down at his feet. He handed the shotgun back to his father bent down and picked up the squirrel's lifeless body and started to cry."

"Oh, that poor little boy."

"Theo's dad reached over and slapped him on the back of the head and said something like, 'Get a grip, kid. That's what life is all about. That animal sacrificed his life so that you could learn how to kill wild game to eat. We'll get a couple more of these and enjoy a fine meal of squirrel stew tonight for supper. Ain't nothing like fresh meat to give a guy the feeling of being alive.'"

"That was awfully cruel."

"I think the humiliation from his dad and his reaction to the dead squirrel sank so deep into his psyche that he swore never to touch a gun for the rest of his life."

Maria leaned over and kissed me on the cheek and said, "Thank you for sharing that. It means a lot. I'll see you tomorrow."

Then she skipped onto the porch and into the house waving good-bye as she went.

Me? I stared for several minutes before driving off. I enjoyed the moment.

Sixteen

Saturday, November Sixteenth

SEVERAL WEEKS AFTER BRIAN'S DEATH, I found out about an interesting incident that made me really suspicious of Santos and his entourage.

It seems that the next day John Santos pulled up in front of a rather colorful house a half block off Eighth Street about a half-mile west of I-95 in Miami. He walked up to the front door of the house and knocked. An elderly woman answered with a big smile and opened the door for him to enter.

The house was large for this particular section of town. One would think that this house should be on a ten-acre lot with an iron gate at the entrance to the driveway. It was an actual replica of a similar house in Havana, Cuba, built by one of the generals that supported Fulgencio Batista, the dictator of Cuba overthrown by Fidel Castro in 1959. The colors were a combination of hues of green and orange in an attempt to capture the colors of the sunset.

As Santos entered the house, he was escorted down a long hallway to a room at the back of the house. The escort opened the door to the room revealing a rather rotund gentleman who commanded so much respect in Little Havana that the people referred to him with affection as El Padrino Gloriosa. He sat at a large desk in front of a window that overlooked a well-kept garden in the backyard.

State Senator Marco Barbosa was in his seventies, overweight, yet in excellent health. He was one of the most respected Hispanic politicians in Florida. He had a cigar in the side of his mouth as if it had grown there. Santos walked across the room to the man who rose and walked around the desk to greet the pastor.

At the same moment, a butler entered the room with a tray of coffee for the two men and poured each a cup full as they met and shook hands.

Santos greeted Barbosa with a perfectly articulated Spanish accent.

"Señor Barbosa, gracias por haberme permitido reunirse con usted."

"Por favor, pastor. Mi casa es su casa."

State Senator Barbosa spoke in perfect English. "You are always welcome in my house, my friend."

He indicated to Santos to sit in an overstuffed chair near the desk. Senator Barbosa picked up a cigar box and said.

"Cigar, pastor?"

The pastor reached over and looked in and said, "Thank you Senator."

As he pulled out the beautifully wrapped and packed cigar, he said, "Havana's?"

The Senator showed a discreet smile and said, "If you tell anyone where you got that, I'll deny it. But of course I do get these through friends in Central America who send them to me through the mail. No money changes hands."

"Thank you, my friend. I shall save this for an appropriate time and place."

"In that case, I'll have Rolando wrap a box for you. It will be ready when you leave."

The Senator nodded his head toward his butler who took the tray of coffee and left the room.

The senator took a seat in an identical chair next to Santos.

Still holding the pastor's hand, he asked, "So, pastor, how can I help you?"

"As you know, the church is in the process of starting a new congregation in Key West with a tent revival."

Letting go of Santos' hand, the senator leaned back in his chair and took a puff on the long, aromatic cigar in his mouth and removed it and trimmed it around an ashtray near him.

"Oh, yes. How is that work going?"

"Well, there's been a bit of a twist. It seems there is a great deal of gossip back here in Miami about me and Brian Silver."

"I'm fully aware of this talk."

"With Brian's murder, we found ourselves in a bit of a predicament. The gossip here is beginning to upset people in Key West, particularly the people in the gay community."

"I'm sure that's causing more problems than the usual difficulties you would be encountering anyway. What can I do to help?"

"I need to know where this is coming from so I can confront it and put it to rest."

"Well, pastor, my understanding is that the two people behind the rumors; well, it seems they have regretted their indiscretions and misrepresentation of a misunderstanding. As soon as I heard what people were saying about you being involved in money laundering and illicit international activities, I knew I needed to take action. I just knew you could not have been involved in any way with what they were saying."

"I appreciate that so much, Senator. I have worked hard to build a transparent ministry here so as to ensure that the people of South Florida could trust in the work that we are doing."

The senator leaned forward and said, "Pastor, I'm concerned about the death of Brian Silver. How is that being handled in Key West?"

"That has complicated our work. I know that many people believe that either I or Marcus or both of us were involved in some way. We have tried to keep a low profile in this matter."

"Do you have any idea who may have done this?"

"Nada."

Leaning forward, the senator said, "Is there any

possibility that--"

"Do I think Marcus could have been involved in some way?"

The elder statesman shook his head in agreement.

Santos continued, "Honestly, I don't think he was, but I wasn't in Key West when it happened. You'll remember I had returned to Miami after the services on Saturday night that ended around nine that night."

"Should I have some of my contacts do an in-depth look into Marcus for you?"

"Not now. If I get any indication at all--"

"You can count on me to take care of whatever you need. Also, let me reassure you that the girl has been looked after quite well. She had a visitor several weeks ago, so I had the Miami-Dade police looking into her visitor. It appears he was only a novelist looking for a story. Anyway, she's in Key West now. You want me to ask the chief down there to look after her as well?"

"No, that won't be necessary. She's working as a volunteer at the tent each night. We'll be able to look after her ourselves. And the author is a local Key West oddity. I think he's harmless. But I would appreciate you calling the chief and telling her what has happened up here."

The senator showed a huge smile and let out a small chuckle. Then he leaned over to Santos and winked his eye and said, "Already done."

"Muchos gracias, Señor Barbosa! How can I repay you?"

With that, Senator Barbosa laughed and said, "Pastor, you have done far more for me than I could ever do for you. All I ask is that you go back to Key West and leave the difficulties in Miami to me. You should work without concern and press on toward building the Kingdom of God."

"You know, Senator, you really should join us in worship at The Christian Center sometime real soon. It would be a huge encouragement to the majority of our membership to see you there."

The elder statesman laughed and said, "You never give up, do you, Pastor?"

"Sir, you understand. That's what I do."

"Perhaps one of these days the Bishop will give me an indulgence to sin and I might walk into one of your services. In the meantime, you leave the politics to me and I'll leave the soul saving to you."

With that, Santos knew he was being dismissed, so he rose from his chair, kissed Barbosa's hand, and left his office satisfied that the problem at home had been taken care of.

He walked to his car and got in on the driver's side. As he put the keys in the ignition, he looked over at the passenger seat and noticed a box about the size of a cigar box wrapped in brown paper and a note that read: "Enjoy."

Santos smiled and started the car, put it into drive, and pulled away with a big smile on his face.

‡   ‡   ‡

LATER THAT EVENING, Marcus Champion and Pastor Santos walked through the tent together as Marcus spoke.

"I feel good about the preparations we've made."

"How are we doing?" questioned the pastor.

"Despite the murder on the last night of Fantasy Fest,

we're on target to break all records for a camp meeting anywhere since Billy Graham."

John smiled as they walked. He then said, "Attendance seems to be strong?"

"You remember the Coral Springs campaign three years ago?"

"Sure."

"Well, we've doubled the attendance of that campaign and are more than fifty thousand dollars ahead of it in giving."

John whistled and shook his head in a rather stunned disbelief.

"I thought things seemed pretty good, but that's terrific."

"That's not the best part. All our expenses were paid up by the third day of the crusade."

John paused overwhelmed. He kneeled down next to a chair and paused for a moment in prayer.

He took a deep breath, looked up at Marcus, and said, "I'm sorry. I was just so overwhelmed by your news that I had--"

"No need to apologize to me, pastor. But that's not everything."

"That's not all?" He said as he stood.

"No. We've taken in enough money to start that mission church here in Key West. I know that was a dream of yours."

"Thank you for all the wonderful work you've done to see that this dream comes to fruition."

"So, how did it go in Miami?"

"Actually, there was no real problem in Miami. It seems I was a bit premature in my concerns. Our friend in Little

Havana took care of everything even before I asked."

Marcus smiled as they continued to walk out into the parking lot and around the area.

After several minutes John turned to Marcus with, "So, what have you found out about our little girl?"

"Not a lot, pastor. Maria's been to see the writer, but she hasn't gone to the police that I know of or have been able to find out."

"I'm not sure what that means."

"It could be she knows nothing. She may suspect some things, but probably knows nothing at all substantial."

"Or?" the pastor questioned.

Marcus stopped dead in his tracks, looked at John, his eyes betraying his concern. He spoke, his voice hard, "Or what?"

"Or, she's planning to talk to us about it all."

Almost with a look of total relief, Marcus picked up the pace of their walking and said, "She's not the blackmailing type?"

"I didn't mean she would try to blackmail me, Marcus. I don't think she's up to causing us any trouble. She's dedicated to the church and wouldn't do anything to reflect badly on her friends. Before she says anything to the police, she'll come to us. All we have to do is wait."

"I hope you're correct," Marcus tried to assure himself more than John. "I'd hate for her to talk to the press. She could hurt us."

"I know, Marcus. But, I truly believe she's not going to do that."

"But--"

John stopped as Marcus took two steps further, realizing John had stopped. So he turned back to face him. John looked at Marcus with a deep concern and said, "Trust me."

Seventeen

Tuesday Morning, November Seventeenth

RUTH WAS SITTING at one of the tables in the open portico of the Ta-Da Club working on her bookkeeping as normal. As she was working, Maria and I arrived on a scooter from down the street. I parked the scooter and we walked into the portico area as Ruthie greeted us, pushing her bookkeeping aside.

"Well, to what do we owe this honor?"

"Ruthie, I want you to meet Maria Hernandez. She's a friend; I mean she was one of Brian's friends from Miami."

"Nice to meet you, darling. I'm so broken up about Brian."

"Thank you so much for saying that. I understand and appreciate the thought. He spoke of you often, that is, when he was home."

Ruthie's face began to turn in a fierce seriousness and said, "I just hope the police catch the S.O.B. that did that terrible thing to him."

"Me too," Maria replied.

We ordered coffee and Ruthie ordered a couple of sweet rolls "on the house" for us.

A few minutes later, Harvey came out of the club holding a cup of coffee. He walked over to one of the other chairs and sat. He pulled out a pack of cigarettes and lit one up. He sat for several moments, took a big sip of coffee then spoke out loud to no one in particular: "Going to be another hot one."

Almost without even listening, Ruth uttered, "Yep."

We all sat for a while in silence enjoying the morning, neither much aware of the other's presence. Maria and I were finishing up the sweet rolls and coffee.

Harvey spoke with no enthusiasm, "Got an idea for a new routine with the theme of Ben and Jerry."

"Oh?"

"Yeah. Thought we might do a sort of ice cream thing."

"Huh?" Ruthie had returned to her work and was not listening to him as she spoke.

"You know, Ben and Jerry's? We can call it something like Ben and Terry's Frozen Delight. Help people feel cooler?"

Frustrated more with a desire to talk to us with some privacy than with what Harvey had offered, she looked up and said, "You work it out and I'll see how it goes."

She looked back at the paperwork in front of her and

winked at us.

Harvey sat for a moment longer then said with an almost faked casual nature, "Okay."

We sat for a while taking in the sunshine and beauty of the morning.

Ruth turned to me and said, "So, how come we haven't seen much of you, young man?"

"It's been hard to attend the shows. Things just aren't the same."

"I know. And now we've lost Ernie. I really liked him. He was not just a good musician; he was a good person. I am still broken up over his death. Do you know how hard it is to find a good bassist? But life goes on, you know?"

Ruthie was never known for showing a lot of emotion except when happy. She was known for her practical, no-nonsense approach to everything in her life. Many people believed that it was her basic attitude that helped keep the Ta-Da Club open and operating in the black, even making a profit during the really tough times.

I acknowledged the wisdom of what she had said and turned my attention to the other man on the porch and said, "How's it going?"

Recognizing the etiquette of the situation, Harvey merely muttered a half-hearted, "Fine."

I turned to Maria and said, "This is Harvey, one of the band members. He played drums for Brian."

"Nice to meet you."

"I think Brian mentioned that you helped him work out several of his routines," Maria said.

Perking up, Harvey smiled, and with a brightness in his

voice, said, "That's right. He was a genius. When he performed, you could see the girl so much that you believed he really was that girl. Brilliance like that comes along only once in a generation." He paused for a moment then said, "I miss him."

"Are you working on anything new?" I interjected.

His eyes darted toward me hard and said, "Got a few ideas. Never know."

"Brian's death must have hit you and the band pretty hard."

Harvey cocked his head slightly to the left and asked, "Why do you say that?"

"I don't know. I got the impression he was a hot item. Crowds picked up when he joined the group. Wasn't there a recording contract in the works?"

"He had a lot of talent. He was fun to work with."

"How?"

Harvey paused again and looked at me as his forehead creased. "He needed very little rehearsal time. He had an ability to get it on the first run through."

"Ideal performer for a band; his loss must have hurt business pretty hard."

"We've had to break in a new headliner. She's definitely not Brian."

"What do you mean?"

"Well, for one thing, she takes too long to get it. And she, well, let's just say she's a real bastard.

"What's his name?"

"Billie, you know? Like in Billie Holiday? But with one tenth the talent. Ain't that a bitch?"

"You seem upset."

Harvey's eyebrows rose high almost to his hairline and let go his emotions a bit like what happened when he threw his drum sticks in the air. But, this time he sat still and said, "Yeah. Brian left us in a lurch but we'll make it. We always do."

At this point, Ruthie jumped in and softened the tension a bit with "No one can replace Brian."

"He was one of a kind," Harvey added as a big smile crossed his lips.

"Someone will come along who'll knock your pants off," I added.

Catching the innuendo, Harvey smiled and said, "Humph."

I smiled as I looked at him for a few more seconds then turned to Ruthie and began to inquire more about the issue before me.

"So, Ruth, what are you hearing about Brian's murder? Anything at all?"

"I wish," Ruthie bemoaned.

"Oh?"

"I've never seen it like this. Nobody's talking. You know how this town is full of gossip? Well, I ain't seen it this tight in decades. Either people know or suspect something big and are afraid to talk, or no one knows anything at all. It's really strange."

I shook my head as I continued, "This murder has got everyone stumped. Even the police have no idea where to go from here."

"Please believe me, Jay. If I hear anything at all, I'll be

sure to let you know, after I call the police, of course."

"Thanks, Ruthie, I'll be back to my usual seat soon."

Ruthie smiled big and pointed her finger in my face like a mother scolding her child and said, "You better, young man! I'm counting on you letting go of some of that money you make off your novels."

Maria and I walked out onto the sidewalk and around to the side of the restaurant, got on the scooter, and rode off down the street as Harvey watched.

Ruthie had already turned back to the work of balancing and justifying her bookkeeping.

Harvey was quiet while staring in the direction in which we left. Then he said almost without any direction at all, "What's he doing? Writing a story about Brian?"

"I'm not sure just what he's doing. I would guess he's planning a novel. That's what he does."

"Who does he think did it?"

At that Ruthie stopped and looked up as Harvey looked back over at her. She stared at him then softened and said, "He hasn't said anything to me about it. But I get the impression he thinks the police are on the wrong track."

"Oh?"

"I'm not sure," Ruthie continued with her gossip, "but I could swear he thinks it was someone close to Brian."

Harvey looked back toward town and said, "But the police announced that they think it was a hate crime."

"Harvey, I'm just an old woman trying to make a living. What do I know about stuff like that?"

Harvey stood, walked out onto the sidewalk, pulled out a cigarette and lit it. He took a few puffs, turned back to

Ruthie and said, "I'm going to go do some shopping. I'll be back for rehearsal at one-thirty."

"Okay," Ruthie replied almost uninterested in him.

Harvey got on a scooter and drove off down Duval Street.

Feeling the effects of the hot sunny morning, Ruthie packed up her things and walked back inside the restaurant and into her cramped little office. If it weren't for the air conditioning, she would never spend one minute in that closet sized room. But in the restaurant business you spend money on the things that affect the customers, not on luxury office space.

I drove down Duval Street and turned left onto Roosevelt. We rode for about a mile or so and stopped in the parking lot of the police station at the Public Safety Complex across from the city marina and basin.

We walked up to the entrance and Maria stopped before the automatic doors could open and asked, "What are we doing here?"

"I need to ask the Chief a few questions."

"Brian never talked about her."

"Well, when it comes to criminals, she's tough as nails. But with everyone else she's very gentle and understanding. Really, you'll like her."

Hesitating, Maria muttered, "Okay," then followed me into the building.

Inside the three-story high reception area, we walked up to the window where a young lady greeted us with a pleasant smile and said, "Hello. What can we do for you today?"

Jay handed her his card through the slot under the glass and said, "I need to speak to the chief for a few moments."

"And what does this concern?"

"Brian Silver."

Her face stiffened as she said, "Just a moment." She punched in a couple of numbers on the board in front of her.

"What was that all about?" Maria whispered.

"Brian's death shook up the police. I'm sure everyone is on edge and treats any mention of the incident with major concern."

The receptionist pushed a button which sounded a buzzer on a door to our right and said, "The chief will see you now. Please pull on that door and walk down the hall. Her office is number eleven on the left."

We entered the interior of the police station and walked down the hall to a door with the number eleven over the title 'Chief' and knocked on a door.

From the interior, we heard, "Come in." I pulled the door open to reveal a rather small, cramped room with a desk, three chairs, and one bookshelf.

As we entered the police chief's office, Fatima stood and greeted me with a firm handshake and said, "Hello Jay."

"Hi chief. This is Maria, a friend of Brian's from Miami."

"You're the girl Brian wanted to marry," Fatima said to her with a smile.

"Si,"

"As you know," I began, "I'm working with Perry on Brian's murder."

"Yes. He told me. What do you have?"

"Not a lot. But I've got some questions."

"Fire away."

"First, what can you tell me about this front man for Pastor John Santos? Marcus Champion?"

"Not much. It seems he didn't exist up until about ten years ago. We haven't been able to find any record of him anywhere prior to that."

Maria's face and eyes narrowed as she mouthed, "Anywhere?"

"Odd, isn't it?" the chief added.

"Yes," I said, "but that answers a lot of questions."

"What have you got?"

"Only suspicions, I'm afraid."

"No hard evidence, huh?"

"No. Not yet. But this guy's very intriguing. I'll let you know what I've found out when I get something."

Okay, Jay. Anything else?"

"Can you give me some background on the band members?"

"Why do you want that?"

"Perry asked me to talk to them. I think it would help if I knew some facts about each of them when I talk to them, you know, to have a little leverage?"

"I'll have one of my detectives do a background search and send what we find over to you ASAP. Was there anything else?"

"Actually, I think that was it. I just needed to have that rumor confirmed. That's all."

The chief stood and reached over to take Maria's hand said, "Nice to meet you, Maria."

Maria stood, took her hand, and shook it. "I appreciate

all you're doing to find Brian's killer."

Fatima turned to me and said with confidence, "We're going to get whoever did this. You call me with anything, including suspicions. Do you hear me, Jay?"

"I sure will," I said saluting her. I took her hand and shook it with, "And thank you, Chief."

"What for?"

"For being good at what you do."

"Hey, how do you know what I'm good at?"

Stunned for a moment, I noticed the twinkle in her eye and smiled real big. I couldn't help but start laughing as we left Fatima's office and walked down the hall and out of the building.

‡   ‡   ‡

I DROPPED OFF MARIA at the hotel, drove to the Key West library, and sat down in front of one of the numerous computers available for public use. I pulled up the Lexus/Nexus research database and typed in the name Ernie Katz.

After about two seconds, the results were displayed on the screen. I began browsing the brief descriptions of each of the search results. I found just twelve articles that had Ernie's name listed. There was nothing in those listing that seemed to indicate anything I did not already know.

I typed in the names of each of the other band members one by one and looked through the resulting articles for each name search. After an hour of reading, I was about ready to give up when an article under the search of Harvey Sims caught my eye.

I pulled up the article titled "Mays-Anderson Wedding" in the Miami Herald society section.

Why would Harvey's name be mentioned in a wedding ceremony article? I wondered.

As my eyes caught the picture of the couple, I hit the print button and walked over to the printer and picked up the two pages that printed out. I walked out the door of the library and sat on my scooter while still reading the article. I sat for several minutes as I read. I whistled, folded the papers, put them in my pocket, and drove off.

‡   ‡   ‡

MY WATCH SIGNALED 6:00 PM as I stopped by Perry's place to show him the article that I had found. However, as I entered, I noticed that Fatima had preceded me by only a few minutes. I shook hands with everyone.

Fatima said, "Doesn't Perry look good tonight?"

"Don't lie to me, Fatima. I look like hell."

"I can't even give you a nice compliment without you spoiling it for both of us."

"Fatima," Perry shook his head and spoke with a gentleness rarely seen in this hard bitten New York cop saying, "We've known each other too long to start lying now. And I know exactly how I look and how I feel. Besides, as long as Theo likes the way I look, I don't care how I look to anyone else."

"I appreciate the sentiment. I'm afraid you'll feel like hell when I tell you what I've come to say. That's why I came right over to let you know instead of attending the meeting I told you about."

"I appreciate that. But, I thought you said you'd call me before you dropped in."

"I did. But something's happened that we need to talk about before we get to what you called me about."

"What?" Perry began in jest. "You've found out that Reverend Santos was a convicted murderer who escaped an insane asylum years ago?"

"Oh, please!" She retorted. "Last night there was another murder."

"I didn't know. I didn't mean to make light--"

"We've been able to keep it out of the news until this morning, which is a lot easier now that Fantasy Fest is over."

"Who was it?"

"Earnest Katz."

"No! Ernie, the bassist? My God! What happened?"

"He was shot through the heart."

"Just like Brian?"

"Just like Brian."

"So, you're telling me about this because he was shot with the same gun?"

"Why do I even pretend to know things you don't know? After you called to invite me over, one of the lab boys brought me the ballistics report on the gun used in Katz's murder."

Perry's forehead was covered with wrinkles and his eyes seemed pale.

"If the same person killed both Ernie, Brian, and may have tried to kill me--"

"And speaking of that, there was just enough marking left on the bullet that hit your door to match it to that same pistol."

"Then this would be the first time in forever that Key West can brag about having a serial killer on the loose. Honestly, I thought I left all that type of stuff behind me in New York City. I mean, small towns are not supposed to be hunting grounds for mass murderers. That's for the big cities," Perry paused, looked at Fatima with deep grooves all over his face, and continued. "Some one's got it in for gays?"

"That's one way to look at it. I mean, it's the first indication we've gotten that Brian's murder may be a hate crime after all. As soon as I get back to the office, we're calling a press conference to announce Ernie's death and make that connection."

"What do you want me to do?"

"Keep on the track you're pursuing. In particular, see if you can find any possible connection between Brian and Ernie other than the band and the fact that they both work at Ruthie's. In other words, just see what you can discover outside the realm of hate crimes."

"Don't you mean between Ernie, Brian and the murderer?"

"That's what I figure. I mean, this whole thing might be a simple problem of jealousy and anger."

"Fatima, jealousy and anger are never simple, especially when you mix murder into the equation."

"Precisely. But pardon my enthusiasm, you said you

thought you knew who the killer was?"

"Yes, but after this news, I've got to admit that I might be wrong. I need to reconsider my theory by giving it more thought and investigation."

Fatima stood to leave.

She turned back to Perry and asked, "Are you going to the meeting tonight? There's still time to make it."

"What's on the agenda?"

"I'm supposed to report on the status of the investigation and that the Christian Center has requested to have a float in the parade next year. It seems that they're not taking any chances in delays this time."

"Troublemakers busy?"

"No kidding. The rumor mill is running rampant."

"Well good luck. I think I'll miss this meeting. I'm just not up for it physically. I'll call Lolita and explain. She'll understand."

"Everyone will understand."

Fatima shook hands with Maria then with me and walked to the gate from the patio and stopped. She stood for several seconds, turned around and looked at Perry hard and said softly, "Perry, how are you doing? Really?"

"Not good. The treatments don't seem to be working anymore."

"Pain?"

"Lots."

"You know--"

"Absolutely."

She stared back at him.

Perry said, "I'll be in touch."

"Bye, Perry. Oh and thanks."

"For what?"

"For being a friend."

"You, my friend, are worth it," Perry said.

As the gate closed on Fatima, Perry lay his head back. The pain seemed to overwhelm him as he closed his eyes. His eye lids puckered from being held shut so tight. He raised his palms up and rubbed his temples with his middle fingers. Theo walked out with a glass of water, leaned over, and handed Perry a couple of pills. Perry started to say something but simply took the pills and swallowed them.

He looked over at me and said, "So, what was it you needed to tell me?"

I pulled the sheets of paper out of my pocket and handed them to him.

"I don't know what this means, but I thought you'd be interested."

Perry looked at the sheets carefully reading them. The he made a low whistle and said, "Oh, my."

Eighteen

Tuesday Evening, November Seventeenth

AT ABOUT EIGHT that evening the large meeting room at the old city hall was packed with people who voiced their anger with loud taunts. Looking back on it all, I wish that Maria and I had attended, but what happened had a profound impact on the case.

Fatima stood at the front with Lolita. She attempted to quiet the crowd but couldn't. Lolita barked out several orders as though she were back in army boot camp where she was a drill sergeant for women recruits during the early 1990s.

She yelled, "Quiet down, people!" Then almost as an afterthought she added, "Please."

A voice in the crowd yelled out in an obstinate tone,

"You quiet down."

"What the hell are you doing to find Brian's murderer?" Another voice blurted out from the back.

"I'm doing all I can," Fatima said hoping to calm the crowd down.

But the noise got so loud no one could hear her.

Lolita had had enough.

"Quiet!" she yelled in such a way as to catch the crowd totally off guard. "Knock it off! Let the chief talk."

The audience became calm and quieted down to an almost deathly silence.

"Please listen to me, folks. We're investigating every angle. This kind of thing doesn't happen in Key West. We've worked hard to make this a safe place."

"What about Ernie?" someone yelled.

"We're aware of that death as well. We've recovered a great deal of evidence that will help us catch his killer, whoever he or she is."

"Bull!" a voice called out.

Fatima shook her head in disgust, looked out at the crowd, and continued, "I know you're not happy with the investigation. And I don't blame you. I'm upset myself. But this killer has eluded us and has left very little physical evidence that we can use to identify him or her. But you could help. Encourage anyone who saw something the night Brian died to step forward. Also, pass the word that if anyone saw anything outside Ernie's apartment, to let us know. Please."

"How would that help?" Lolita seemed to voice what everyone else was wondering.

"We haven't found anyone who will even admit to being near Sloppy Joes the night Brian died. If anyone saw anything, we need to know. And no one has admitted being anywhere near Ernie's place. Even if someone saw a car or a scooter anywhere near his street. I mean anything that was out of place or there for the first time; that kind of information could help us find the person or persons that did all this."

"We know who did it." Another voice yelled out. "It was those tent people down here from Miami. They hate gays."

Others in the crowd began to echo the sentiment, "Yeah! They did it!"

Fatima tried to speak above the crowd but found that she was now unable to either calm the noise or calm the crowd. Just then, the crowd noise subsided, so she quickly spoke up.

"There is no evidence the people from The Christian Center were involved in any way with the murder of Brian or anyone else in the city."

At this point, a familiar voice was heard loudly.

"Why don't you ask that preacher man where he was on the night Brian was killed?"

"Yeah!" Someone called out. "Make that preacher talk."

"Who is that out there saying that? What do you know about the preacher? Come forward so we can talk."

The crowd grew silent and people looked around. No one admitted saying anything.

"This is what I'm talking about. If people won't speak up so we can investigate, we'll get nowhere."

The crowd remained silent.

"If you won't do anything about those church-loving freaks, then we will!" Someone cried out breaking the silence.

That got the crowd yelling and sounding very obstinate and angry. No one was paying attention to Fatima any longer. There was yelling and people calling for everyone to march on the tent meeting.

Another person yelled out, "Let's go teach those people some respect."

And the crowd started leaving the meeting room.

Fatima turned to Lolita and said, "Let's go."

They exited out the rear door as the people in the crowd started yelling for the chief to resign and leave town. The two got into the chief's car.

Fatima grabbed the radio microphone and called for an alert to a possible mob action at the Old City Hall. She also told the dispatcher to have the sheriff send a crowd response unit to the location of the tent revival for a possible disturbance.

She changed tone and said, "Calvin, make sure you alert all patrol units. Hell! Call everyone. Put out a general alarm!"

"You mean everyone on duty?"

"No. Everyone."

"People are asleep. They'll be pissed."

"Dammit, wake 'em up and tell 'em to meet me at the revival tent in the park."

"Are they at Little Hammock Park?"

"No, Calvin, they're in the park in front of the Eco Center. Now, call them. It's an emergency. Break out the riot gear and meet me there as soon as you make the calls. Oh, and Calvin, move your ass!"

Lolita turned to Fatima and said with a sound of urgency, "Honey, these people are our friends. But, I don't recognize them at all. Oh, God, what's happening to our wonderful little town?" Lolita broke into tears.

Fatima could not break down. She had to keep her head and get people in the best places to stop any possible problems.

"I feel the same way, Lolita. I just can't understand what's happened. But, we're not going to let anyone get hurt. Do you hear me? Nobody gets hurt."

The crowd moved outside the community center in an unusual scene, even for Key West. Several hundred gays walked together yelling and screaming for the head of the tent preacher. And yet, nearly everyone in the crowd wouldn't have known the man if they saw him.

A strong, authoritative voice was heard yelling out, "Let's go get that murdering son of a bitch!"

The crowd answered, "Let's go!" And they marching toward the tent revival location with yells of "Yeah! Let's go. Kill them all."

Fatima and Lolita drove off with lights flashing. A few minutes later, the cruiser pulled up and stopped in the parking lot of the revival tent. The lot was empty, the meeting having ended about a half-hour before. Fatima and Lolita exited the car and went to the door of the motor home parked next to the tent and knocked.

"Open up. It's the police."

"What's going on?" yelled someone from the inside.

"Please. Open up. It's an emergency."

The door flung open and Marcus stepped out. Through the open door, Fatima could see John sitting at a table in some kind of conference with a couple of other people.

She looked at Marcus and said, "There's a pretty nasty crowd coming and I'm not sure that I can stop them."

John Santos rose, walked to the door, looked down at Fatima and asked, "What's going on?"

"Some very influential people believe that you are responsible for the murder of Brian Silver."

"Heaven help us." John whispered as if praying. "What should we do?"

"I only have twenty officers on the force. And I'm not sure just when they'll be here. I've also alerted the sheriff's department and they're sending several units here. Hopefully they'll arrive in time."

"I appreciate you coming to warn us, chief. But we had nothing to do with any murder, especially that of Brian Silver. He was my friend. I couldn't have harmed him in any way."

"Maybe so. But I need to ask both of you where you were on the night Brian was killed."

"I was in Miami. At home," John replied.

"And I was here completing plans for the tabernacle crusade," Marcus admitted.

"I assume you can prove where you were?"

"The last place I would be," Marcus snapped, "is in the middle of that debauchery downtown. I have a reputation to guard."

"I understand all that. But I must ask you if you can

prove where you were?"

"No. I didn't know I would need an alibi."

Fatima replied with a simple nod and a look of suspicion but understanding.

John added, "And my wife can vouch for me. A lot of people saw me in Miami during the evening."

"Okay," Fatima continued. "So, tell me, Pastor Santos, just how do you know Brian Silver?"

"He was a member of our church in Miami."

"John," Marcus interjected, "maybe you'd better tell her everything."

"What do you mean?" Fatima asked.

John seemed reluctant as he said, "I'm originally from Cuba. Migrated twenty years ago. I was young and wild."

Marcus encouraged him. "Tell her, John."

"Brian is my son. It was a one-night fling in Havana. A girl named Juanita. I left Cuba because her father was going to kill me."

Marcus attempted to mitigate the situation with his words, "If this had gotten out; well, you understand?"

"So, when Brian came to America, he came to you and told you he was your son and you took him in?"

"Actually," Marcus answered, "we helped him find his own place as he became active in the church. That's all."

"He came to Key West," said John, "to take a job singing for some lady who offered him work in her club."

"That would be Ruthie at the Ta-Da Club," Fatima offered.

"Unfortunately," Marcus added. "The type of singing he did was--"

"Embarrassing?" Fatima finished his sentence.

"To say the least," John continued.

"A perfect motive for murder," Lolita offered under her breath.

To which Marcus retorted, "Who did you say you were?"

"She's helping me with this investigation," Fatima explained.

John took control of the situation as he said, "It looks terrible, but I supported his work. He was engaged to be married to a young lady in Miami."

"There was no animosity," Marcus added.

Hearing the sounds of the crowd approaching Fatima turned and said, "Thank you. I'll see what I can do with the crowd."

"It's a good thing all the people who came tonight have gone home," John added. "This could have been really nasty."

But before Fatima could leave, John added, "Oh, and chief?"

"Yes?"

"Thank you." And John offered his hand.

She took his hand, squeezed it tightly and shook it.

"It's my job, Reverend."

As Fatima and Lolita stepped out into the parking area, they saw that several police officers were standing near the entrance to the tabernacle tent. As the crowd approached down Southard Street, the police showed their weapons.

The crowd stopped about fifty yards away and yelled out invectives and called for the pastor to come out. As the adrenalin began to flow causing her face to feel hot and red,

Fatima walked out to meet the crowd.

"Okay, people," she said as her voice began to crack from the heightened emotions welling up inside her. "Break it up right now! I am not your friend, I'm the Chief of Police. I'm charged with keeping the peace. So, listen to me. Go home, all of you. There's nothing here for any of you."

"They hate us!" someone yelled from the crowd.

"You don't know that," Fatima attempted to answer.

"They murdered Brian!" another yelled.

"Listen to me! I've investigated these people. They had nothing to do with Brian's death."

"Go to hell!" Another voice yelled out.

"Damn it!" Fatima yelled as she began to show her anger and frustration. "You people go on home. Please."

"We deserve justice!"

"I'll find Brian's murderer. I promise! Trust me."

"Why should we?" Another voice yelled out.

"You know me. I've never let you down before."

Several people began chanting, "We want justice! We want justice!"

"I know." Fatima yelled over them, "So do I. Just let me do my job."

The audience began to settle down a bit as Fatima continued.

"You all know me. I'm one of you. We've done so much together. Please. Give me a chance. I promise justice will be done."

There was a pause. The crowd began to move away a few at a time at first then more and more as Fatima watched.

In a quiet voice that betrayed her deep fearful emotions,

Lolita said to Fatima, "Wow. I never expected that to happen."

"Uh, look to your right," Fatima said pointing to five distinctive, green striped sheriff cruisers with deputies wearing riot gear of bulletproof vests, helmets, with shotguns drawn, standing beside their vehicles.

Lolita smiled as her voice reflected the relief she said, "That was a close one."

"They may be gay, but I really didn't want to tangle with them."

"And I guess they didn't want to mess with those guys. So, what's next?"

"I just hope to God that Perry comes up with something very soon so we can put this whole thing behind us."

Lolita pointed to the cross on top of the tent, and said, "Maybe we should say a prayer? You know. Just to be sure we cover all our bases."

Fatima looked at her with a smile and put her arms around Lolita's neck and said, "I love you so much, silly girl."

They walked together to the cruiser. Lolita got in the passenger side as Fatima walked over to the deputy sergeant and thanked him for being so timely in his arrival. The sergeant signaled for the deputies to return to their duties. Fatima shook his hand and he got in his cruiser and drove off.

Fatima walked over to her lieutenant and said, "Thanks for the quick response, Calvin."

"Just following orders, ma'am, uh, Chief."

He signaled to several of the officers to let them know

they could go home. He turned to two officers next to him and said, "You two stay here for a couple of hours just to be sure everything remains quiet."

He turned to Fatima, saluted, got in his cruiser, and drove off. Fatima walked over to her car and got in.

"Is everything okay?" Lolita wondered aloud.

"I think so," Fatima replied.

Lolita sat in silence as Fatima started the car and pulled out.

Nineteen

Thursday, Early, November Nineteenth

IT WAS WELL AFTER MIDNIGHT and in the Monument Street Café Maria and I sat at my regular table, me with a huge hamburger in my hands. Maria sat across the table watching me eat.

She shook her head in disbelief, leaned over, and said, "That's a lot of food for so late at night."

"I know," I answered with a muffled voice as I stuffed my mouth full of hamburger, onion, tomato, lettuce, bun, mustard and ketchup, "but I have to eat when I'm thinking."

Maria sat and watched me continue to eat until the very last piece. I even licked my fingers and took a big gulp of cola.

Maria said, "So, what do we do next?"

"I don't know."

A bit taken aback by my statement, Maria shook her head and said, "You don't know?"

"No. Yes. I do know."

"What then?"

"I'm going to wait here."

"For what?"

"I'm really not sure."

"You're not making any sense."

"I know."

"We're just going to wait here?"

"Yep."

"And what are we--" she stopped in mid-sentence. "Oh, yeah."

"Actually, I don't know."

"So?"

"How will I know when it happens?"

"Yeah."

I looked into her eyes and with all the seriousness I could muster and told her, "I'll know it when I see it."

I put my hands to my cheeks and creased my forehead in thought. I took a pen out of my pocket and began to doodle on a napkin.

After several minutes, I looked up and said to Maria, "Have you tried the hamburgers here? They taste pretty good, for hamburgers. I don't eat much red meat, but I'll eat their hamburgers."

"Jay! We can't just sit here."

"Why not?"

"The murderer may be getting away."

"I don't think so."

"Why? I'd run."

"It's already been two weeks. If he, or she, hasn't left yet, he's not going to leave. He feels safe."

"So who do you think is the murderer?"

"I wish I knew. I mean, it could be any number of people."

"Like who?"

"Well, there's Pastor John."

"Pastor John? Do you really think he could have killed Brian?"

"I don't know. He's hiding something. People have been known to kill to keep secrets."

"But he's a pastor."

"And your point is?"

"I've known Pastor John for years. I just can't imagine."

"What about his sidekick?"

"Marcus?" Maria said, "Well, he's another story."

"Could he kill someone to keep Pastor John's secret?"

There was a long pause and a puzzled look on Maria's face.

"Okay. Maybe he could. But if he did, it wouldn't be with Pastor John's knowledge."

"Maybe so."

"Who else could have done it?"

"Let me ask you a personal question first."

"What?"

"You and Brian had been seeing each other. And weren't you planning on getting married?"

"Yes."

"Had you noticed any changes in Brian's action over the last several weeks of his life?"

"What do you mean?"

"Did he seem less interested in you as before?"

"What are you saying? That Brian was gay? That he was using me to cover up?"

"No."

"Because he wasn't," she insisted almost in tears, "I would know."

"Of course you would."

"So, don't even think that."

"But maybe people around here might think he was."

"These people are crazy. Brian wasn't--"

"Crazy?" Jay interjected.

"Gay."

"But, what if someone close to him started thinking he was. Or maybe wishing he was."

"So?"

"Then he finds out that Brian is not." When I said that, I had to stop and think for a moment. I started, "I mean--"

"Oh God," Maria began to cry. "He might have been murdered by someone he knew."

"It seems the evidence could indicate that."

"How?"

"There were powder burns. He was shot up close."

"Brian is so trusting," added Maria.

"Was."

"What?"

"Brian was so trusting."

Straightening up with a seriousness that scared me,

Maria said in a stern voice, "Don't patronize me."

"I'm not, but it seems you're not facing the reality of Brian's death."

"Give me a break. You're a writer, not a psychiatrist."

"Touché,"

"No. Yes. No, I mean. I didn't mean; okay. I guess I am having a little difficulty with Brian's--"

"Death? Listen, Maria, he was trying to get started in his singing career. He wanted to be taken seriously and--"

"And this was the only way he felt he could do it? I mean, how does a poor Cuban boy break into the music business in America anyway?"

"He was Cuban?"

"Yes. Didn't you know?"

"No. He gave no indication--"

"He was ashamed of not ever getting the proper documents after he arrived. He told me once that he believed he didn't have legal status because he came in on a boat by night. He never went to the immigration office to declare his status as a Cuban refugee."

"Oh. No one knew?"

"Only me. Oh, and Pastor John."

"How did he know?"

"I don't know. But there was a connection there."

"That's it. Let's go," I said as I stood and put some things back into my pockets.

"Where?" She asked.

"Ruthie's place."

"Wait, Jay, it's nearly 2:00 AM."

"Oh yeah. Okay. I'll take you back to your hotel and pick

you up at ten in the morning."

"And what are you going to do?"

"I've got to talk to the band. Maybe they're still around. The show ended about an hour ago."

"In that case, I'm going with you."

We walked out of the restaurant and drove off down to Ruthie's club where the light was on in the front office. Ruth was sitting in her usual place at a table in the open air bar as we drove up on the scooter. The place was still wide open and Ruthie looked out to see who had driven up.

"Well, what are you two detectives up to this late at night?"

We walked into the bar area as I spoke to Ruthie, "I got a couple more questions I want to ask the band members about Brian."

"Sure, honey. But first maybe you two better come with me to my office where we can talk without being disturbed."

We walked in the front door and into the office to the right. The room was small and cramped with all kinds of posters and other memorabilia from the acts she had developed over the years. There were a few old books and a lot of file folders laying around on the shelves and on the chairs. Ruthie had made out a small area in the middle behind the desk where she worked on her bookkeeping.

As we cleared two chairs and sat down, Ruthie started. "Most of the band members left several hours ago. I cancelled the show tonight because the guys wanted to go to the community meeting. So, what is it you want to know? Maybe I can help you?"

"You knew Brian pretty well."

"I was like a mother to him."

"Did he have any special friends?"

"What do you mean? Special or 'special'?"

"Was he close to anyone? You know spent a lot of time with anyone in particular?

Ruthie thought for a moment or two and said, "I can't think of anyone at all like that. He seemed to be friendly with everyone."

"Think about it, could be anything such as maybe some constant interactions with other people."

As if on cue, Harvey stopped at the office door, looked in and said, "How is everybody doing?"

"Fine," I answered. "You still hanging around?"

"We went to the meeting tonight, but I left early so I could get some work done here. I needed to clean up my dressing room. I'm going to grab a nightcap, home, and then to bed."

"Harvey, don't be late for rehearsal like you was yesterday, you hear?"

"Yes ma'am. I'm sorry about that. I got jammed up with some stuff. It won't happen again."

"Well, you been doin' pretty good, so far. Don't worry about it."

"Bye," Harvey said.

He went out the front door and walked down Duval Street toward the pier area.

Ruthie watched out the window as he walked down the street. That's when she wheeled around and said, "I'm getting worried about that boy."

"Ruth, Harvey's no boy," I chimed in.

She chuckled a bit under her breath then looked at me with a twinkle in her eye and said, "Sweetheart, when you get to be my age, all the men are just boys."

"I've learned that already," Maria interjected, "and I'm not even thirty.

"Jay, there's one thing I just thought of," admitted Ruthie.

"What?"

"It's just an impression, but that voice I heard in the dressing room? Well, it sounded familiar, like I knew the person, but I just can't place it. You know? With all the noise."

"Is there anything else like a look or exchange or anything?"

"I may sound quite paranoid," Ruthie stuttered.

"What?" I encouraged.

"Well, there seemed to be a lot of interplay between Brian and Karl several days before his death."

"What do you mean?"

"Like part of the act, you know?"

"I'm not sure. What?"

"It's kinda like, well hittin' on each other, you know?"

"Karl was hitting on Brian?"

"No, I don't think so. It was kind of like it, you know?

"Let me think about that. It could have just been part of the act. Anything else?"

"Jay, I swear, everybody loved Brian," Ruthie said as tears began to roll down her face. "He didn't have an enemy in the world."

"Someone had it in for him. I have some questions to ask

the band."

"They have a rehearsal here around five tomorrow afternoon. Come by then."

"I appreciate it. We'll be back. Bye."

"You take care. Okay?"

We got up, walked out onto Duval Street, and got on the scooter. I decided to take Maria back to her rooming house. Just then, I heard the blasts of several fire trucks headed toward the western end of the island.

"I hope nobody's house is on fire," Maria said.

"Probably just an auto accident."

We drove down the several blocks on Duval and turned right on Fleming. As we approached the hostel, I stopped the scooter and Maria got off and said, "Well, I guess I'll see you in a few hours. I can't believe it's after two in the morning."

"I know, I'll pick you up for lunch at around eleven-thirty, okay?"

"Sure. I'll see you then."

Maria looked up toward the southwest and pointed to a small stream of smoke in the air. "Look, is that somebody's house or something?"

I looked back over my shoulder and saw the smoke.

"It sure looks like it."

"Hurry!" Maria encouraged. "Let's go see what it is." She jumped back on the scooter.

Reluctantly, I drove off on the scooter across town. It was so late that there was no traffic. I got a sinking feeling in the pit of my stomach as we got closer to the smoke indicating a bad fire. We turned on Southard and up to the parking lot where we expected to find the tabernacle tent.

Instead we found fire trucks with lights glowing filled the tent parking lot. And the tent? Burnt to the ground along with the furniture. There was nothing much at all left but smoldering ashes where there was once a large circus-type tent filled with chairs and other types of equipment.

John and Marcus were standing near a fire truck. We drove up, parked the scooter and walked over to where the two leaders were located.

I spoke first, "Pastor John?"

"Mr. Morrison. It's gone."

"¡Aye Dios mio!" Maria remarked.

"¡No sé lo que pasó!" Pastor Santos added.

"Who did this?" I asked.

"We have no idea. No one saw anything. But I wouldn't be surprised if it weren't someone in the crowd that was here earlier tonight."

Stunned, I inquired, "What crowd?"

"We had a bit of a confrontation here," Marcus answered.

"A lot of people were upset with our being in Key West preaching the gospel." John added. "They wanted to shut us down. But, the police stopped them. And we thought they all left. A couple of policemen stayed for about an hour, after which they left."

Marcus continued, "But it looks like someone took matters into their own hands and burned the tent. I suppose they thought we'd just pack up our bags and go home. But I'll tell you this, that won't happen!"

"There was no reason for this," I said.

"Amen, brother!" John added.

Fatima walked up to us and said, "Reverend John, I'm so sorry about this. I can't believe someone came back and made a mess of things like this."

"Thank you. But you showed us what you're made of when you faced those people a few hours ago."

"Key West is a gracious city full of friendly people. I'm so sorry, but I guess there are a few people who are a bit too possessive and just don't get the real picture of what our civilization is all about. Our country is free for all to live and practice as they wish. Unfortunately, there is always a particular group of people who think everyone else should live the way they want them to live."

"Seems like some people haven't gotten the memo about being nice," Marcus added.

"We'll find who did this. I promise you!"

"Like you've done with Brian's murder?"

"That was uncalled for, Marcus," John said as he turned to him with a stern look on his face.

"I'm sorry, sir. I—"

"No offense," Fatima said. "We're all tired and angry. Let the fire department clean up here. We'll all feel better in the morning."

She turned to John and said, "If you're interested, I'll see if I can locate another spot or another tent so that you can continue your revival services."

John and Marcus looked at each other in stunned silence. John said to Fatima with a sort of gasp in his voice, "You've taken my breath away."

"I'm not converting," Fatima said to him, "I just feel it

necessary to show you how nice we can be here. What happened to you tonight has never happened here, ever."

Marcus stared at her for several moments then whispered, "Damn."

"What?" Fatima responded with shock.

"No. Yes. I, I guess I'm just, well, overwhelmed. I mean, you're a, well, uh--"

"A dyke?"

Marcus stood with his mouth still open.

Fatima smiled at him and reached out to touch his arm and said, "I know who and what I am and I'm not ashamed. Are you?"

Continuing to be a bit shocked, he recovered and said to her with a kind and gracious tone, "Of course not. I was just taken aback there for a moment that--"

"That a gay person could be human?" Fatima interjected.

Marcus continued to stare and think about what had just happened. He reached out his hand to Fatima and said, "Pax?"

Fatima looked at his hand, smiled, took it in her hand, and shook it with a simple word, "Pax."

"I know you've been looking into my past and discovered that I didn't exist too far back."

"I had to check. That's my job," Fatima replied.

"I know. I immigrated here illegally. I'm not a citizen."

"We both came over here from Cuba," John added.

"John took me in and helped me establish a new identity after I arrived."

You're Cuban? Well, you're legal because of the wet-foot/dry-foot policy."

Again Marcus acted stunned.

"What?"

"I know a good attorney here in Key West who can help you obtain legal status with a green card and a chance to become a full-fledged citizen of the USA." Fatima wrote on the back of her card and handed it to him. "Here's his name and phone number."

Marcus stood acting as if in disbelief as he said to her, "I don't know what to say."

John leaned over to his ear and said, "You might try 'Thank you.'"

They laughed out loud together.

John relaxed.

"We've got a lot of work before the services later tonight. It'll be sun-up in just a few hours."

"I'll see what I can do," she concluded and shook their hands.

Fatima and Lolita walked toward the police cruiser. John and Marcus stood watching for a few moments as the two women drove off.

"Why didn't you tell her the truth?" John asked.

Marcus shrugged his shoulders and walked toward the remains of the mobile home. The police began putting up yellow tape as the firemen sifted through the rubble of what once was the tabernacle tent of The Christian Center of Miami.

I leaned toward Maria and said, "Let's go."

As we walked, Maria pulled on my shirt and said, "What's the big hurry?"

"I've got a bad feeling about this whole thing."

"What do you mean?"

"I'm not sure. All I know is that I think we need to go now."

We got on the scooter.

Fatima called out to me.

"Drive carefully!"

"We'll see you tomorrow," I replied.

Then we drove off.

Twenty

Thursday Morning, November Nineteenth

AT ABOUT SEVEN, I awoke to a pounding on my door. I quickly put on my pants and discovered a young man in a suit standing on my porch. I opened the door and said, "May I help you?"

The gentleman showed me his badge and handed me a file folder with several papers in it. With a smile he said, "The chief asked me to drop this off to you. Is there anything else you need from us?"

"Is this the report on the band members?"

He nodded in the affirmative and bid me farewell.

I walked back into the house and was astounded at what I found in the file. So, I immediately called Maria and asked that she meet at the restaurant to go over what I had received from the chief of police.

It was nearly 10:00 am as we sat together scouring through the papers from each of the file folders, I learned much more about Brian and the other member of the band. Even Maria was a bit surprised at the almost squeaky clean records on each man.

Maria admitted, "I'm so proud of Brian. He has had no run-ins with the police that I can see here."

"Yea, I noticed that as well. He's almost an ideal for any Boy Scout Troop. Well, except for the dressing up like a woman thing."

Maria flashed those eyes at me in such a way that I continued, "No offense meant. I just couldn't pass it up."

"I know. But, really?"

We continued reading through the files for several minutes as we sipped on our coffee and ate the Danish I had ordered for us to share.

Looking through Nelson Williams' file I stopped and let out an almost silent whistle.

"What is it?" Maria responded.

"Nelson, the rhythm guitarist? He was busted for drug possession."

"No. I mean Brian always spoke so well of him."

"Let me see what it says here. He had a reputation as a master guitarist among the Atlanta music scene, having played with several major pop and rock bands in the area. He was born at the Baptist Hospital downtown and grew up in a small house on Harvard Avenue in College Park. It's weird, but I know where that street is."

"What? You do?"

"Yes. It's near Hartsfield International Airport. I can

picture him rising early in the morning as the planes would land and take-off over that house. I know I'd have never gotten over the rumble of jets as they lowered their wheels right over my head."

"Is that a nice neighborhood?"

"Oh, no! I'm sure that most of the homes along that area are torn down by now."

"So, I guess he overcame his neighborhood and became a successful musician."

"Let's see. Nope. He did that after the drug thing. It seems he got involved with a group of men who were picked up in a drug raid in the apartment complex where he was living. It seems he spent a year in the county lock-up for drug possession, a charge to which he pleaded guilty hoping to get off with no jail time. It was his first offense. It looks like the judge decided it was time someone received a big sentence rather than agreeing to the plea agreement."

"Oh, wow. That's awful. What happened?"

After that experience it seems he kept himself clean and away from people like those he had hung with. He concentrated on his playing; but since his jail time hung heavy over him, he found it difficult to find work other than playing in low class bars for fifty dollars a night."

"That's so sad."

"I know. I'd imagine Nelson had every reason to be bitter and blame everyone else for his arrest. It looks like he took responsibility for his actions since he admitted he had bought the drugs he had on him. No one stuck it in his pocket. So, I suppose he dedicated to become the best guitarist he could be. He was playing in Atlanta's

Underground when Ruthie introduced herself and invited him to move to Key West and play guitar in her band."

"A real success story there."

"I don't think we have to worry about Nelson."

Maria leaned over the table and picked up the file folder with the name "Odell Lewis" on it and said, "So what about this guy? What's his story?"

"Now, there's a man with an amazing story to tell. Odell can be classified as a true delta blues man born and raised in Mississippi in a small community outside Senatobia called Coldwater. Odell knows what real poverty is like. He and his mother lived in a little shack on Arkabutla Road just outside town. And would you believe that his mother was a domestic working for two families in town. And yet, Odell was a good kid. He helped his mom with the house work as he dreamed of becoming just like the blues singers and guitarists who would play the back road dives for a few dollars a night."

"That was his dream?"

"It seems so. There's an article in the file where he gave an interview to a reporter from *Rolling Stone Magazine*. In the article, he recounts that there was a hell-hole bar called The Place that was located about five hundred yards down the street from the house where he lived. He said that the management had hired a blues band to play on the weekends. So, on Saturday nights, he'd sit out on the front porch and listen to the music coming from the open doors and windows of the little building. When he turned thirteen, his momma gave him a guitar she got from a local pawn shop. I think the article mentions that she paid two dollars."

"Two dollars?"

"Yep. A flat top acoustic it was. When she handed it to him he recounts that she said, 'Now, honey, I can't pay for no lessons. So you'll just have to figure it out on your own.' So, He would sit on that porch and work at sounding just like the guitarists in that band. Later he inquired of the owner if he could come in and practice with the band. The owner listened to him play and immediately told him to sit in with the band on rhythm guitar."

"Now that's the makings of a movie."

"Maybe so, except there is no prison time or horror. He was a straight arrow and gained the reputation in the music world as an honest, hard-working guy who simply loved playing music. About five years ago, Ruthie heard him playing outside of a hotel in Memphis and bought him a one-way ticket to Miami where she picked him up a few weeks later and brought him to Key West. And that's all there is to tell about Odell."

"There doesn't seem to be anything in these files to indicate any problems."

"I haven't found anything at all. I mean there was an incident with Harvey Sims. But it wasn't his fault."

"What incident?"

"Well, let me give a synopsis of the entire file. I think it will help me to distill the information for myself and save you a lot of time reading through the material."

"Okay, but will it take a long time?"

"Not really. Let me see. Harvey Sims was born and raised in San Diego a child of the eighties. He was the third of five and I guess felt most of his life that he was almost forgotten in nearly everything that was going on. When he had had a few too many, he would tell people the story of the time that he and his family had gone to Disneyland when he was nine years old. As the family was leaving the park to go home, they got through the gates and were waiting for the tram to the parking lot when his mother exclaimed, 'Oh My God!! We forgot Harvey.'"

"No way! They really forgot their own son?"

"There's a copy of an incident report on file with The Disney security people in the folder. When they showed up with Harvey in tow, they handed him over to his family. Then his father began to blame him for being lost and making them have to worry and wait until he was found."

"His father blamed him?"

"Seems impossible, doesn't it." Although his family had plenty of money, they never spent it on their children or allowed them to have money without earning it by working in the family business. Well, it seems that Harvey was extremely judicious with the money he earned. When he turned fourteen, he asked his parents if he could take drum lessons. First they laughed but finally agreed that if he would practice in the basement of the house, he could buy his own drum set. But there would be no lessons unless he could pay for it."

"His parents sounded so cruel."

"And yet, he seems to be a fine man today. But, to continue, every night Harvey would bang on the drums where no one could hear him playing. Over the next year he did not realize it, but his skill as a drummer was increasing in amazing ways. He would learn to play the hit music of the time by playing along with records and tapes attempting to mimic the drum players he could hear."

"He seems to be really good on the drums; from what I've heard."

"When he graduated from high school, he asked his dad to give him some money to move to Los Angeles. His father agreed and gave him $2,000 to get settled in the big city. But, he said he would have to pay it back. When he arrived, he was able to find a room to rent and got a job playing drums in a small studio band that did back-up for aspiring singers."

"Sounds like he was on his way to becoming a success."

"One day after playing most of the day and listening to some really terrible singers; and this is where it gets really interesting; Harvey and a friend walked a half-block to a bar they frequented to have a stiff drink to forget his headache and maybe pick up some girls. Well, one of the men that they had accompanied earlier in the day was in the bar and began to have some words with Harvey and his friend over whether or not the band was causing him to sing poorly. Harvey said very little until he just stood up and hit the man so hard he fell over backward and hit the floor with a thud. He lay there unconscious for what seemed to be several minutes."

"No!"

"Everyone in the place was so stunned at what Harvey had done that they just stood there without saying a word. The poor guy on the floor finally shook his head several times, stood up, and walked out the door. A few minutes later he returned with a police officer and accused Harvey of assaulting him. But no one in the place would corroborate his story."

"They all lied?"

"Yep. And after the policeman left, everyone laughed. The singer pulled a gun and shot at Harvey who ducked out of the way. The policeman ran back in yelling at the man to drop the gun. When the gunman turned around, he pointed his pistol at the officer who immediately shot the man killing him on the spot."

"What?"

"No kidding! And soon after the inquest ended, Harvey decided that he needed a complete change of scenery and a new beginning in life. He moved to New York City for a couple of months following Christmas. But, realizing he couldn't stand the cold weather, he started looking for another place to live. He was reading the New York Times and saw an advertisement for musicians to perform in Key West. He called the number in the ad and bought an airline ticket."

"Just like that?"

"Yep. After arriving in Key West, Harvey met up with Ruth at the Ta-Da and was immediately hired after she heard him play at an audition she was holding. He got a small apartment on Stock Island and bought a scooter to get around."

"Wow. No wonder Brian liked him so much. He would tell me all about Harvey and how much he depended on him. He once said he was the only person he could depend on to keep a perfect rhythm going no matter what. And that's key to a dancer and singer."

"But the problem," I added, "is there's nothing here to

indicate that anyone in the band would ever do anything to Brian or even have any idea why Brian would be murdered."

We sat there for about another hour then left since we wanted to grab the opportunity to at least give the members of the band a chance to share whatever they might know.

I was disappointed. I thought for sure there would be something in those file folders that would give us a clue as to why Brian might have been killed. There was nothing. In reality, the files seem to indicate that Ruthie had assembled a group of angels to be her performers.

Twenty-One

Thursday Afternoon, November Nineteenth

LATER THAT AFTERNOON Maria and I stood in the middle of the main hall of the Ta-Da Club where about a hundred tables and six hundred chairs were all set up for the evening's entertainment to start later that night.

Karl walked in and stopped as he saw us standing there. He called out to us, "Can I help you?"

"I'm Jay Morrison."

"Oh, you're the one Ruthie told me about. You wanted to talk to the band members?"

"Yes. I'm looking into Brian's murder as part of a tribute I plan to do about him. I want to get the band members' take on Brian. You know. What was he like? Who were his friends? Was he good to work with? You know, the regular stuff."

"I thought the police were looking for someone from the Christian community for Brian's murder."

"Oh, I didn't mean I was investigating the murder. I'm putting together information on Brian's background, you know. I'm doing it because he was my friend."

"Oh, yeah," Karl added then walked over to the piano and sat down.

I watched him take his seat. I asked, "Where is everyone else?"

"Oh, this bunch of guys ain't much for doing what they're told, except for playing music, of course. They'll all show up eventually."

"Okay, what can you tell me about Brian?"

"Didn't know him other than he did a hell of a job doing Barbara and Madonna. I mean, he wasn't that much of a musician or even that good of a singer, but man he could make his voice sound like almost any female singer. He was what we refer to as a vocalist."

"You never talked to him about his life?"

"Nope. Didn't care to."

"What did other members of the band think of him?"

"You'll have to ask them."

"I'm asking you."

"Look, man. These are musicians. They ain't drinkin' buddies or nothin'. When we get together, we're rehearsing for the show or jamming. You understand?"

"Okay," I said as I changed tone and strategy, "You hear talk, don't you? I mean what kinds of things have you heard, you know, around?"

"Well, I'm not one to talk--"

"Hey. I know."

"Well, I think Harvey sort of had a crush on him, if you know what I mean?"

I became interested and Maria gasped almost in silence.

"Why do you say that?"

"I heard 'em arguing in the dressing room every so often."

"Harvey was in Brian's dressing room?"

"Almost every night for about a month before, you know. I figured they were just good friends."

"Where did Harvey come from?"

"I don't know. I think he came here from Miami, but then just about everyone here went to Miami first, you know?"

"I didn't."

"I didn't mean--"

"It's okay. Did you know Ernie very well?"

"I should. He and I were lovers."

"I'm so sorry. I didn't know."

"We had a brief service yesterday before he was cremated."

"You don't seem too broken up over it."

"I don't go around showing my emotions all over the place in public, you know? I cry at home."

"How long was he with the band?"

"Several years? When Ruthie had to fire Bo Phillips for being drunk before performing, she hired Ernie as our bassist. He and I became pretty close. It was like we really clicked, you know?"

"On the night Brian was killed, did anything unusual happen?"

"Naw, man. Not that I remember. Why?"

"I'm just trying to piece together what happened, you know, for my article. That's all."

"One thing weird, though. Ernie and I were supposed to go out after the show was over to have dinner then go to the parade. I guess he got done putting away his stuff early because he was waiting out in the hallway when I came out of the green room. I thought he would come in to let me know he was ready."

"Is that near Brian's dressing room?"

"Yeah, across the hall. Wait a minute. As I came out into the hall, I overheard Brian and Harvey arguing again. You know, like screaming and stuff in there. Harvey came pushing out of Brian's dressing room and shoved Ernie out of his way. Ernie told me later that they were yelling at each other in the dressing room for several minutes."

"Did he say anything?"

"No. Yes. I think he said something to Ernie like, 'What the hell do you want?'"

I thought about that for a moment. "Did Ernie answer him?"

"No. I think I said something like, 'We're going out to dinner. What's it to you?' But, that's all."

"Did he leave after that?"

Karl paused then said, "No, I think he hung around awhile."

"Did he leave before you and Ernie left?"

"Hmm," Karl thought, "He was still backstage when we

left."

"Had that ever happened before?

"What?"

"Harvey and Brian screaming at each other?"

"I don't think so. At least, I never heard it. Usually they were joking around a lot. That's all. No real yelling."

"In your opinion, does Harvey wear his homosexuality on his sleeve, or does he hide it?"

"Harvey is sort of a closet gay; he comes out when he thinks it's safe or if he thinks he might have a chance with someone. You know? He isn't feminine, if that's what you're asking."

"But on that day they were arguing?"

"That's what I said."

"So, where's Harvey now? Do you know?"

"Hell if I know. He's been late for rehearsal almost every day since Brian died."

"What about last night?"

"Last night? We didn't play last night."

"Didn't you have a rehearsal?"

A bit puzzled, Karl answered, "Last night? There was no rehearsal last night. We all went to the meeting. Harvey was there, too. In a sense he led the meeting. He marched with us all the way out to the tent church. He seemed to be in charge."

"Oh god!" I breathed.

Maria touched my arm.

"What is it?"

"Why didn't I see it?"

"See what?"

"Harvey," I said. Then turning to Karl, I continued with my voice sounding as dispassionate as possible, "Thank you, Karl. I'll come back later to talk to the others."

"Anytime, my friend."

Maria and I left the hall and approached the scooter. I stopped and turned to Maria with, "I can't believe I've been such a fool."

"What are you talking about?"

"Harvey."

"What about Harvey?"

"We've got to get to Perry's right away."

"What are you talking about?"

"There's no time. Hop on!"

We mounted the scooter and drove down Duval Street toward Perry's apartment.

As we were driving, Maria yelled over my shoulder, "Stop! Stop this thing now!"

I pulled the scooter to the side of the street and turned off the engine. I turned my head around just as Maria got off the scooter.

"Jay, what the hell's going on? Tell me."

"Don't you see it?"

"See what? I don't understand what's going on."

"Harvey."

"Harvey what?" Maria pleaded.

"It's been Harvey every step of the way."

"Harvey's been where?"

"Harvey's been at the center of throwing suspicion to John and Marcus."

Maria looked at me through a blank stare.

So I continued, "It was Harvey who suggested to the gay community that this must be a hate crime caused by someone connected to The Christian Center. And I'll bet he was behind the burning of the tent to distract and even confuse the investigation."

"I still don't see it. I mean, I thought John and Marcus were the ones we were supposed to be looking at, or at least one of them."

"Harvey was the one to distract everyone. He even got Perry misdirected. He lied about last night. He wasn't cleaning up his room. He was leading the crowd to the tent. And remember, he left us in plenty of time to get to the tent and burn it down before we ever got to your hotel. Oh God. I hope I'm wrong, but I think he killed Brian and Ernie both."

"Why do you think that Harvey killed Ernie?"

"Remember that Ernie was standing outside the door of Brian's room? I'm sure Harvey saw him standing there after they had that argument. I'll just bet Harvey wanted to make sure that if Ernie put two and two together and come up with him as Brian's murderer, well I think he felt he had to stop him."

"Why do you think Harvey was not at the club last night like he said he was? I mean, we both saw him there."

"He was never at the club until he slipped in through the back door to give himself an alibi, with us!"

"Oh, wow. I--"

"We've got to find Perry and tell him all this now."

I pulled out my cell phone and called Perry.

Perry answered the call sounding rather weak. "Yes?"

"Perry, this is Jay."

"Oh, hi Jay."

"Listen I've got to talk to you. Where are you?"

"Theo and I are on our way back from Miami. I had some treatments today. We should be back around six. I'm not sure I'll feel up to company, but you're welcome to stop by."

"Listen, I think I've solved this thing, but I need to pass the theory by you and see if you agree."

"Okay, Jay. That'll be fine. Drop by after six. That'll give me a chance to rest a bit before you arrive."

"I'll see you in a few hours."

Twenty-Two

IT WAS FIVE-THIRTY, Perry sat relaxing on the back patio. The sky shimmered between a light blue to an aqua with a slight breeze in the air while the sun set into the darkness of the Gulf. The temperature was perfect for an evening on the patio in November. Theo came out from the house to where Perry was reclining.

"Perry, I'm heating up some hot chocolate. You want some?"

Perry strained to look up at him. He was pale, weak, and suffering from the recent round of treatments.

"That sounds great," he struggled to say.

Theodore started straightening up a few things on the table beside Perry to make a place for the hot chocolate.

While moving things around, he heard a rustling noise coming from the area outside the gate.

"What was that?" Theo turned toward the gate.

"What?" Perry asked.

"I don't know. I thought I heard something. That's all."

"You've been jumpy lately, my dear."

"I can't help it. I mean after that incident; you know? The gunshot and all; it's just more than a person can handle."

"I know. But there really isn't any need to worry about it. If we run into any trouble, I have Lucy here to help us out."

He reached under his blanket and pulled out his nine millimeter Glock.

"Please," Theo said, "Put that away."

"This thing has helped me out of many a scrape over the years. I trust it."

"I can't help it. I'm worried. I mean, you're so weak."

Perry reached up, took Theo's hand, and squeezed it. Theo looked down at Perry.

Perry said, "Go fix that chocolate."

Theo looked down at Perry with a sternness not normal for his face. He allowed himself to take a deep breath and turned to leave. But he stopped, walked over toward the patio gate, and checked to see if it was closed and locked.

He threw the lock over the handle where someone trying to open the gate from the outside would find it difficult to reach through and manipulate. Theo checked it twice to make sure it was secure.

Perry shook his head with understanding and placed the pistol back under his blanket within reach of his right hand.

As he leaned back in the chair, he opened up a book to read just as Theo passed by his chair on his way into the house.

He heard Perry in a quiet voice say, "Satisfied?"

Theo stopped dead in his tracks and looked down at Perry. He stared at him for a moment then broke into laughter. They both laughed for several moments after which Theo walked into the house shaking his head.

As Theodore walked from the patio into the house, Perry lifted the book, turned to a page marked with a small thread, and started reading. Out of the silence the rustling sound as before drifted onto the patio. This time Perry heard it and perked up.

"Is someone there?"

The wind chimes began to tinkle in the soft breeze that drifted in from the ocean.

He looked over at the chimes and laughed a moment, and he said, "I'm getting as paranoid as Theo."

Then he turned back to his book sliding his hand under the blanket and patting his pistol.

Theo was at the stove stirring a pan of hot chocolate when a shadowy figure began to creep toward him. Oblivious of the movement, Theo turned on the radio, switched to a CD that was already loaded, and turned up the music. The sounds were familiar and reminded him of his childhood in South Louisiana.

Just then there was the sound of a soft thud and Theodore crumpled to the floor unconscious. A hand reached over and turned the burner under the hot chocolate to the off position. That same hand reached over and turned off the light in the kitchen and turned up the volume on the stereo. The intruder worked his way back into the dining room and to the door out to the patio.

Perry stopped reading, marked his place where he ended and placed the book on the table to his right. He leaned his head back against the pillow behind his head. He looked exhausted and pale. His eyes started to close as he spoke aloud.

"You know, Theo, I think that hot chocolate will hit the spot before Jay and Maria get here. Just set it down on the table. I need to sit here with my eyes closed for a few moments."

The shadowy figure crept up behind Perry, a red scarf gripped in each hand. He came closer and closer to Perry in near total silence. Perry opened his eyes with a concerned look on his face and leaned over toward the kitchen window and noticed that the light had been turned out.

He called out, "Theo! Where are you? I thought you were bringing the hot chocolate out here."

There was no sound. Perry tried to stand but was so weak he couldn't.

"Where are you, Theo? Theo, answer me. This isn't funny!"

In the alley leading to Perry's apartment Maria and I arrived and parked the scooter next to the entrance to the garage. We got off the scooter and walked to the front door. I rang the bell and waited for a second or two then rung it again. I pushed the button again and could hear the bell ringing in the house, but there was no response from inside.

A moment or two passed when I heard the soft tones of Perry's voice calling, "Theodore! Where have you gone? I

263

thought you were making hot chocolate. And now the doorbell is ringing. Can you at least answer the door?"

I turned to Maria and said, "Theo's coming to the door."

The sounds of rustling came from the back patio which caused me to jerk my head up. "What was that?"

"What?" Maria responded.

"I thought I heard something around back like someone calling out, but muffled. Let's go check."

We rushed around to the back patio entrance and tried to open the door. It was locked. I looked through the bars and noticed that Perry was not in his usual chair. I tried to put my hand through the bars but it was too big. Maria reached over and put her hand through and slipped the lock off the handle.

I pushed the door open and rushed inside ahead of Maria. As we entered through the gate, we saw someone choking Perry.

I yelled out, "Hey!"

The figure looked up. It was Harvey. I lunged forward to grab him but he threw a punch that knocked me to the ground dazed. Harvey continued to pull the scarf in the choke hold on Perry. I looked around and grabbed a metal chair nearby and swung at Harvey, but Perry lurched sideways in an attempt to free himself. Harvey fell with him and I swung in vain.

Grasping the immediacy of the situation, Maria pulled out her cell phone and called 911 telling the dispatcher to rush help to Perry's house.

Harvey's hold on Perry was too much as the old NYPD detective began to lose consciousness. I jumped at Harvey grabbing him around the shoulders. We struggled as Perry went limp. I pulled hard against Harvey finally causing him to lose his grip from the scarf. As he let go, I was able to loosen the scarf from around Perry's neck. Harvey pulled a pistol from his pocket and pointed it at me.

As I felt an excess of adrenalin causing my heart to pump hard against my chest, I balled my left fist and knocked the weapon from Harvey's hand, sending it sliding across the floor. It stopped out of sight among the bushes behind us.

I jumped at Harvey hitting him hard in the stomach as I wrapped my arms around him. We struggled against one another, fighting to try and get the other in a choke hold. But we both were too quick as we changed positions in a constant winding motion.

I realized that even though this guy often acted mild-mannered, Harvey was muscular and much stronger than me. So when he made a move to get his arm around my neck, I ducked and rolled away from him.

At that moment a hand reached out and picked up the pistol that I had knocked out of Harvey's hand.

Even though I had pulled away, Harvey was quick and able to get behind me and get a choke hold around my neck. Harvey grabbed the red scarf he had brought with him and wrapped it around my neck. He was just too fast for me and pulled hard on the scarf.

I struggled against the stronger man's grip but realized I was weakened by the intense fighting. My pupils began to pull upward as I gasped for breath. I knew at that moment that I was ready to pass out. And there was nothing I could do about it.

Just then a loud bang echoed through the patio. I felt the grip around my neck weaken as Harvey faded and fell forward almost in slow motion to the ground behind me.

Shaking off the fog in my head, I threw back the scarf, rushed to Perry's side. He was not breathing. I started CPR, pressing down hard on his chest. Fear shot through my whole body as I realized that Perry was not responding. I continued to push on his chest.

Perry coughed a few times and began to struggle against me as if he believed he was still being strangled. I grabbed his shoulders, looked into his eyes, and said, "Thank God! You're alive. I thought we had lost you."

Perry was gasping for breath. He shook his head.

I sat back on the floor and leaned against the large chair that Perry had been seated in before the struggle. I looked at my friend.

Then we both looked over at Harvey who was lying on the floor not moving.

"It was Harvey!" I said.

"That's who you wanted to tell me you suspected?"

"Yes."

"Looks like you were right."

"Well, it never crossed my mind until just before I called you. That's why we arrived early. He was always ahead of us keeping up with our investigation and seemed to anticipate our every move. That's what I wanted to tell you when I arrived."

We both looked over at Harvey's body lying beside us on the floor. Perry smiled at me and said, "You could have told me that over the phone," causing us both to laugh aloud. Perry fell backward exhausted as if passing into unconsciousness.

I shook him saying, "Perry, you've got to stay awake until the EMTs get here. I don't want to lose you."

Perry replied in a weak voice, "I'm okay. I just can't sit up. Just let me rest here until they arrive."

"Sure," I replied, "Just relax. But don't close your eyes."

Remembering Maria, I turned toward the house and saw Theo standing frozen, leaning against the door into the dining room with the smoking pistol in his hand. Tears were rolling down his cheeks as he held tightly to the one thing he swore he would never use. I slowly stood to my feet and made my way over to him struggling to stay erect. I placed my hands over his and took the pistol from him.

I watched as Theo slid down the glass door to the floor sobbing like a little baby. I bent down and put my arms around him and in a soft and gentle voice said, "I know. I know."

Maria had the telephone in her hand as she looked over toward where Theo and I were located and said, "The police and paramedics should be here any minute."

I watched as Theo sat with his back to the door. I slid my back against the door and sat on the floor next to him. I leaned back and closed my eyes for a moment exhausted.

Theo said, "Perry?"

"He's alright."

Theo leaned his head against the glass door and closed his eyes for a moment and whispered, "Thank God."

"No," I replied, "Thank you, my friend."

Theo sat there with tears streaming down his cheeks as he said, "I'm too tired to argue."

I closed my eyes again, reached over and patted the back of Theo's hand.

Maria had made her way to where Perry was lying, sat next to him and placed his head in her lap as she spoke to him, "Just keep looking at me. You've got to stay awake. Please, Perry, don't take your eyes off me."

In the distance, we heard the sounds of sirens as they approached closer and closer.

‡   ‡   ‡

ABOUT AN HOUR LATER, the police seemed to be everywhere. There were patrol cars in the alley in front of Perry's place. There were several cars behind the place with lights flashing red, blue and yellow. Fatima and the county sheriff were both standing in the garden area looking at the body that the coroner's assistant had placed on a gurney, wrapped in a black plastic body bag.

Fatima shook her head as she looked down. Almost as if to no one in particular she uttered, "Harvey Sims. Who'd a thought it was him?"

The sheriff looked at her and in an effort to comfort her said, "There's no way you could have known who Brian's murderer was. It could have been anyone. Besides, all that matters is that he was stopped before he could kill anyone else."

"I know. But poor Ernie didn't do anything except be in

the wrong place at the wrong time."

The paramedics worked on Perry who was now sitting up in his wheelchair.

One said to him, "You've had a pretty bad shock to your system. And considering your present condition, I think we need to take you to the hospital to make sure the injuries are not worse than they appear, you know; just to be on the safe side."

"I don't need to be in any damn hospital."

"Sir, it's important to check you out from head to toe. So, please go with us."

"If I go there I'll never come home."

The paramedic sighed and handed him a clipboard with a paper on top and said, "I think you're making a mistake. But, I need you to sign this refusal of service affidavit, if you don't mind."

Perry signed and handed it back to the paramedic who replied, "Please take it easy Mr. Savant. And don't hesitate to go to the hospital if you start feeling woozy or like you might pass out."

Perry looked at the man with a slight smile, "Of course I will, son."

The paramedics finished packing up their things and walked out through the gate to the street where they turned off the truck's emergency lights and drove off.

Fatima walked over to Perry and said, "My God. I only wanted you to do a little investigating, not take on the murderer all by yourself."

"That's all I thought I was doing: just investigating."

"Who'd a thought it would be Harvey?"

I chimed in with, "Actually, it all makes sense."

"How?"

"His questions, his militant desire to cause problems for the Christian Center people. All that should have tipped us off."

"I was so stupid not to see it all." Perry spoke up.

"How? No one else saw this coming."

"I thought perhaps Harvey might be involved," Perry added almost as if apologizing, "But instead of having Theodore take me to the police station to discuss my suspicions with you, I decided to wait here until you called me back. I was just too exhausted to do anything at all."

Fatima added, "I'm so sorry, Perry."

"There's nothing for you to be sorry about. It was my decision. I felt so safe with Theodore here. I should have been more cautious."

Theodore walked out of the house and into the backyard with a bandage on his head.

"I never saw it coming," he said holding his hand to the bandage on his head.

"I can't believe I put you in such danger, my dearest!"

Theo turned to Perry and touched his shoulder.

"This was not your fault," I added. "Harvey did it all by himself. He's the one to blame for everything."

"I know. But I still feel bad about it."

I walked over to Theo, placed my hand on his shoulder and said in an almost apologetic tone, "You'd better tell him."

Theo looked terrified and shook his head.

"Do you mind if I tell him?"

Theo looked at me and nodded as a tear rolled down his cheek.

Perry inquired, "What are you two plotting?"

I looked at Perry and said, "I think you need to know something."

"What?"

"It's about Harvey's death."

Perry looked puzzled and said, "You shot him before he could choke me to death. Right?"

"Uh," I stammered, "Actually, I didn't shoot him."

"What?"

I looked back with a slight smile. Perry looked over at Maria who held up her hands and indicated a "no way" shake of her head. Perry gasped out loud with a look of shock and dismay.

"Theo! You?"

Theo stood as if frozen to the floor. He lowered his head almost ashamed and uttered under his breath, "Yes."

Perry looked at him with an almost cold, dead stare. Then with a detective-like voice he said, "You killed Harvey Sims?"

Theo nodded his head just a little as he looked at the floor.

"You saved my life?"

Perry opened his arms really wide, smiled, and said, "Come here, you big oaf."

Theo rushed to his arms and slumped down crying like a little baby as Perry hugged and kissed his head and cried.

Fatima slipped next to me and pulled me aside.

She said, "When Theo started working for Perry as his

personal assistant, he tried to teach Theo how to shoot so that he could be his bodyguard. But Theo was so deathly afraid of the weapons. It seems something happened to him as a kid. I don't know what that was. I assume that he told Perry the story because he promised Theo he would never ever have to pick up a gun again as long as he was with him. At least this was Theo's decision and not Perry's."

"Actually, I think I know the story. He must have been horrified to discover that he was going to have to shoot Harvey if he was going to save Perry from a sure death sentence."

"I can't think of what he must have gone through at that moment. It must have taken every ounce of energy and strength in his body to pull that trigger in enough time to save Perry's and your life."

"I hope that I can find a woman who can love me as much as Theo loves Perry."

"You and me both, my friend."

I turned to her with surprise written all over my face. That's when we all broke out into laughter.

Perry and Theo both looked up as Maria came over and hit me and Fatima both on our shoulders.

"Ow!" I said, "What was that for?"

Fatima looked shocked.

"This is neither the time nor the place for laughter, you two."

I looked over at Maria and replied, "You're right. I'm sorry."

Just then Perry spoke, "So, what about Harvey?"

"Harvey must have been so jealous of Brian he felt he

needed to so something drastic," I replied.

Fatima added, "I guess when he found out that Brian was only acting like he was gay, he must have snapped."

"Perhaps he might have thought that Brian was ridiculing him," Perry added.

I turned to Fatima and said, "That makes sense to me" as Fatima nodded her head in agreement.

She added, "He used the gay community to cover up his crime by trying to get everyone angry at The Christian Center people."

Theodore added, "Nothing positive comes when you use violence to solve your problems."

"Amen, Brother!" Perry added. Then he turned to Fatima and asked, "What about the tent revival?"

"Of course, the tent was burned down last night. They lost everything. So I arranged for city workers to clean up the lot and replace the tent, lights, chairs and sound system just in time for tonight's meeting."

Maria looked at her with glee and said, "You what? Oh my God. You are the best."

Maria gave Fatima a big hug.

Perry looked over at Fatima and said, "I'd like to attend the service tonight; you know, to add my support."

Shocked, Theo looked over at Perry and said, "What? Perry Savant going to church?"

Fatima added, "Maybe we should all pay our respects and show support for visitors to our fair city."

Maria added, "John Santos is a fine preacher. You won't be disappointed."

"I'm going out there in a few minutes," Fatima offered.

"To check to make sure everything is working well."

She turned to Perry and Theo, "The services will be starting around seven-thirty tonight. You guys can ride with me, if you want."

Theo smiled and said, "I just hope Reverend Santos doesn't faint with all the gays in the audience."

Perry reached out to me and pulled me over to him and said, "Jay, thank you."

I reached over and took his hand and shook it.

"Thank you for getting me involved in this."

"I've got a feeling we're going to see a phenomenal novel about Key West's first honest-to-god serial killer. What are you going to call it, the 'Impersonator Killer'?"

I thought a moment then said, "How about 'Death on Duval Street?"

"Uh, Jay, nobody was killed on Duval Street." Theo added.

We all looked over at Theo and stared for a moment then broke out in laughter at this tall young man's innocent honesty.

At that, Lolita walked into the room and put her arm around Fatima and whispered in her ear. Fatima looked at her and said, "Right. So if you're going with me and Lolita to the revival service, we're leaving now."

I looked around stunned and said, "Are you guys serious? You're going to the tent revival? For real? Tonight? I mean, I haven't had a chance to go home and change clothes. Look at me."

Perry interjected, "Why not? Doesn't Jesus believe in the phrase, 'come as you are?' I'll bet he's the one who invented

'BYOB!'"

I paused. "Let's see if the roof of that tent falls."

Theodore pushed Perry a few feet when Fatima stepped up, moved him out of the way, and took the wheelchair. "Allow me the honor."

Theodore backed off as the others started out the door.

I stood stunned.

Theo turned to me and said, "Well? You're the church guy; aren't you going?"

I smiled. "This is one church service I wouldn't miss for all the gold in world. Let's go."

Theodore walked over and gave me a great big hug and kiss on the cheek.

"What was that for?"

"You are--" He paused. "Just because."

We walked toward the door. Maria stood smiling. I turned back and said, "Hey. I need someone to ride on the back of my scooter."

At that, Maria started to laugh and ran to take my hand as we all walked out the door.

Twenty-Three

Thursday Night, November Nineteenth

INSIDE THE TENT, the people filled the seats to near overflowing. John Santos was all smiles as he moved among the people while they entered for worship. It was as if he knew that attendance would be over-flowing tonight. The sounds of "Onward Christian Soldiers" could be heard coming from the sound system as the band at the front played a rather upbeat version of the hymn.

Outside the tent, the parking lot was filling fast. Instead of a few volunteers directing the traffic, uniformed police officers were working alongside the volunteers, showing people where to park. The excitement seemed to permeate the air as people exited their cars with smiles carrying their Bibles with them. The atmosphere was almost carnival-like.

Fatima guided her police cruiser into the parking lot with lights flashing and stopped at the main entrance. She parked just to the side of the large doorway into the tabernacle tent. Fatima, Lolita, and Theo slipped from the car and opened the trunk from which they pulled Perry's wheelchair.

Theo opened the back door and helped a weak but smiling Perry Savant from the car's backseat with great care. He slipped him carefully into the chair as Fatima shut the door. Lolita, Theo and Perry entered the tent as Fatima got back into the cruiser and moved it out of the way of the pedestrian traffic.

Maria and I pulled into the parking lot, parked the scooter in a spot next to Fatima's cruiser, dismounted, and joined the others as we entered the tent.

Theo wheeled Perry down to the front row where he sat with Perry in the aisle beside him.

Before she sat, Lolita looked over at the other side of the tent and said, "Will you guys please excuse me. Hold a chair for me. I'll be right back."

She walked away toward the back and across to the other side. A few moments later, Fatima, Maria and I sat on the row behind Perry and Theo.

Fatima leaned forward. "Where's Lolita?"

"She'll be back in a minute, so hold that chair for her," Theo whispered.

We all sat there almost unnoticed for several minutes when John Santos walked up to Perry and reached out his hand.

"John Santos is my name. I assume that you are the detective I can thank for catching Brian's murderer."

Perry reluctantly took John's hand and shook it.

"News travels fast in this town. But first I must say I didn't catch Brian's killer, he caught me. The honor of stopping that man from killing more people goes to my best friend and the love of my life, Theodore Prejean."

Without batting an eyelash, John turned to Theo and extended his hand to shake. Theo sat for a moment then stood and took John's hand with a firm grip.

John smiled and said, "I am deeply grateful for your help in this matter. Brian was a member, uh, Brian was my son."

Theo looked at him a bit puzzled; then he smiled and said, "I didn't want to hurt Harvey, but he was trying to kill Jay and my dear Perry. I had to stop him."

"I don't presume to speak for God in such matters; but I think He understands more than we do. You were protecting your friend. Anyone would have done the same thing."

Blushing, Theo released John's hand and said, "Do you think that maybe God will forgive me for what I did? I mean, I took a human life. That's a mortal sin."

"Are you a man of God?"

"I believe that God exists. I was raised Catholic in South Louisiana."

"My friend, God sees the heart and knows yours. I'm sure He has already forgiven you because of your willingness to sacrifice your belief and yourself in order to save the life of one you love so much. I mean, isn't that what Jesus did?"

At this, Perry pushed himself up and stood on his own.

He looked eye to eye with John and said, "Reverend Santos, you're a bigger man than I had thought. I was never fully convinced that you had anything to do with Brian's death, but I had to investigate. That's why I sent Jay to talk to you. I had to be sure. I hope you understand."

At that John opened his arms and said, "May I?"

Perry stepped forward a bit shaky and the two men hugged. Theo stood there as he reached up and brushed away a tear.

Fatima leaned over to me and said, "If I never did before, I think this moment would convince me that God really does exist."

"Me, too, Fatima; me, too," I whispered.

As Perry sat carefully back into the wheelchair, Marcus stepped up and shook everyone's hand.

He reached for my hand and said, "Thank you for all you've done."

I looked at him for a moment, stood up, reached out and shook his hand.

After taking my hand back, I handed Marcus a folded couple of sheets of paper and said, "I thought you might like this as a souvenir of my investigation."

Marcus looked puzzled at first. He stared at me. He lowered his head and opened the two sheets of paper. His shock was apparent on his face as he saw a copy of a newspaper article about the Mays-Anderson wedding. As he looked at the other sheet he saw another article about the CEO of a local savings and loan who was arrested for embezzlement. At the top of the page was a picture of a man being led out of the bank in handcuffs.

Marcus' went totally void of color as he looked at his own face in the picture. The face of the groom in the one article was the same as the man who was being arrested.

He raised his head and stared with a hard look at me as I continued, "I was doing a little research on the hunch that you might have had a past or maybe had met Harvey somewhere. But both?"

Marcus tried desperately, but was unable to keep his face from betraying the deep concern welling up inside his belly. But he held his composure and said, "I honestly had not remembered that Harvey had played in the band for the reception. Plus, I was exonerated of that--"

"Marcus," I said interrupting with a gentleness that bespoke of the kindness I felt in my heart. "Your secret is safe with me."

Marcus' face turned from an embarrassment to a look of anger as I continued to speak.

"John Santos is a good man. Perhaps even a man of God. He deserves much better than you as his personal assistant. So, if you ever cause any problems with my friends here in Key West, or if you bring any disgrace or cheat on Reverend Santos; well, I think you get my point."

A smile crept onto Marcus' face as he reached his hand to Fatima.

Still looking back at me, he gradually turned to the chief of police, and said, "Chief, you have gone beyond the bounds of normal duty in making all this possible. Thank you from the bottom of my heart."

Fatima stood and grabbed Marcus' shoulders and gave

him a huge bear hug.

"You're welcome, friend."

At that moment, Marcus realized that she was unaware of the past that I had discovered.

Just then, a young woman approached us and whispered something to John. After a moment, he turned to us and said, "It's time. We need to begin."

Pastor Santos walked up to the front of the audience and the worship service began with everyone standing and singing the opening hymn in loud and exuberant sounds of joy.

Marcus looked back over to me and whispered, "You have nothing to worry about. I believe God has used you to remind me of what is truly important in life. Thank you."

I looked into his eyes and smiled as he nodded his head. At this point, I reached over and gave Marcus a strong hug around the neck.

A moment later Lolita walked up and pushed her way to her seat next to Fatima who turned and said, "Where were you?"

Lolita put her finger over her lips and pointed to the other side of the tent. Fatima turned to see what she was pointing at and there, sitting together near the back, sat thirty of their friends from the gay community.

"They all showed up to show support for you and the spirit of goodwill and cooperation."

Lolita indicated to Jay and Marcus to look their way.

Fatima bent down and whispered something in Perry's ear. He turned and looked at her with a huge shocked look on his face. He pushed hard and stood with everyone else in order to look over to the other side of the tent.

At this moment, the song had ended and everyone started sitting down.

John Santos walked to the lectern at the front and said, "Ladies and gentlemen. The past several days have seen an incredible series of events for which I feel we need to stop and give thanks. First, if you have not already heard, the person who committed two heinous murders and the attempted murder of another here in Key West has been caught. And justice has already been carried out.

"This man also was responsible for the damage to the tent and our equipment here. But thanks to the gracious help of such people as our chief of police, we have this beautiful new tent and all these chairs and other equipment, which I believe belongs to the city of Key West. I cannot express just how deep my gratitude is for such kindness. But I can recognize those who helped. Would everyone who helped in putting up the tent and moving everything in and setting it all up please stand and allow us to thank you?"

At this, ten men near the front dressed in city maintenance suits stood. Fatima and Lolita stood followed by thirty variously clad gays on the other side of the audience. More than eight hundred people began applauding with great enthusiasm. For a few minutes in Key West, peace reigned at the most unusual meeting ever held in the history of the city.

Reverend Santos stood quietly for a moment as the applause died down.

He said, "My friends, I want to tell you a brief story. It's all about a man who loved God very deeply, yet had a talent that no one within his group of friends understood or recognized. So he fled his home in order to pursue his dream related to his talent. Within a year he had become one of the great performers in his field.

"Despite his extraordinary success, many of his friends could not understand or accept just what had happened. Then in a fit of rage, a very jealous person ended his life tragically and senselessly. And still, people could not accept who or what he had been.

"Then God did something He had not done in a long time. He sent a messenger of peace and love to the friends this young man had known years before. And just like John the Baptist, the people who needed to hear the message got distracted by what the messenger appeared like. And just as the people around John the Baptist, they were ready to hurt the messenger rather than heed the message.

"I'm proud to say that this congregation has received that message loud and clear this evening. As one who needed to hear this message, I want to share with you what I have learned. I may not agree with a person's actions, lifestyle, or preferences in life, but as a representative of Jesus Christ, it is my duty to show everyone around me the love that Jesus showed me. It is my duty to my God to look beyond the exteriors and see the heart in need of God's love. It is my duty to speak less to the areas of disagreement and emphasize the areas of need.

"Jesus never told us to clean up the sinner before bringing him to God; he said we must bring that person to God first then let God clean up the person as He sees fit."

Reverend Santos walked down the ramp to the floor and

over to where Fatima Sax was sitting and indicated with his arm for her to stand. She did with reluctance as her face seemed to turn a bright shade of red.

He turned to the audience and said, "All of you know our chief of police. She was a highly decorated police officer in Miami. She made public her sexual orientation when the Dade County Sheriff announced that she would become the new chief of police in Key West. I was outspoken in my opposition to her because she was gay. My opposition to her lifestyle is a stand for which I am not ashamed because I am not ashamed of my personal beliefs about homosexuality. But today I stand before you with a new understanding of just how God's love manifests itself in our lives.

"I am still opposed to Fatima's sexual orientation because it is my belief her lifestyle is not what God intended. But I also recognize that God showed His love for us in that while we were all sinners and disagreed with everything we were doing and living, Christ died for us. If God can love someone like me, as sinful as I am, then, I have a responsibility to show others that same love no matter who or what they are."

Reverend Santos reached over and put his arms around Fatima and hugged her. The place was filled with stunned silence. Tears flowed from the eyes of people all across the sea of humanity that filled the tent.

Marcus stood up from his seat on the front row and walked over to Theo and stuck out his hand. Theo hesitated for a moment with a look of wonderment. He stood to his full height and grabbed Marcus with a huge bear hug. At that the entire place broke out in applause.

Everywhere people shed tears of joy and others turned and hugged one another in pew after pew. Then a couple of people near the back of the room walked over and started to hug several of the gays seated nearby. After that people all over began to sing the first stanza of the old hymn, "Just as I am without one plea."

The noise of people talking and crying subsided as the singing spread from person to person with the choir finally joining in the chorus, "Oh, Lamb of God, I come; I come."

I sat for several minutes looking around me. Then as if a light of understanding came on inside, I turned to Maria with a twinkle in my eye said, "Did we just witness a miracle?"

‡   ‡   ‡

LATER THAT EVENING, Theo, Maria, Perry, and I were sitting in Perry's backyard enjoying the cool evening atmosphere of the patio. The wind chimes sang together in a cacophony of differing tones and timbres.

Perry seemed more alert than he had been in weeks. He expressed himself with, "Wow! This whole evening was invigorating. I haven't had a good tussle like that since I left the force. If I had had my strength, I'd have whipped that young man's ass."

Theo chuckled out loud.

Perry looked over at him with, "Oh, you think that's funny?"

"Perry, darling, you're a pansy and you know it. So just

admit it."

"Well, I guess Key West has made me pretty soft in my old age."

"Well I think you did a great job," I added. "You obviously scared the hell out of Harvey. Otherwise, he would never have taken the chance to try and kill you."

"I know," Perry responded, "In a sense, it scared me more than I've been scared in my life, especially when I realize that there was no way I was going to be able to fight that guy off. I've never felt so weak and helpless."

Maria chimed in, "Perry, if it weren't for that disease, you really would have given Harvey the fight of his life."

"That's sweet, dear."

"I believe in you, that's all."

"Now, Theo. Did you hear that? You should be jealous of this girl. She's sure throwing the compliments around."

Theo smiled and winked at Maria said, "Yeah. I guess I should be. But then, I know you, Perry, and I'm not afraid of her; Jay, maybe, but not her."

"Hey," I said, "don't drag me into this triangle."

At that we all laughed and had another drink.

About the Author

HERB SENNETT's career as a writer began when he turned sixty-five. Although ready to retire, he wanted to fill his last several decades contributing to the joy of reading.

He has a long background of teaching communication and theatrical arts first as a high school English, speech, and drama teacher before moving to the college classroom in 1985. He holds degrees in education, communications, theater arts, and religious studies. His final degree, a Ph.D., is from LSU.

Over the past twenty years, he has written two academic books, three major screenplays, and two stage plays. He has been recognized for his scholarship and creativity in the academic and entertainment worlds. He is listed in *Who's Who in America* and is a retired army reserve officer with service in the Vietnam War and Operation Desert Shield/Storm.

Herb's first novel, *The Reluctant General* was published in January 2014 through Westbow Press, a subsidiary of

Holman Publishers. It recounts the story of Deborah and Barak from the book of The Judges in the Christian Bible. He is currently working on a follow up novel based on the story of Gideon. He has plans to continue the series covering other major figures of the Bible.

Death on Duval St., Herb's first mystery novel, is based on a character named Perry Savant who was forced to retire early from NYPD following a series of rumors that hit the headlines. In his new home of Key West, Florida, Perry helps local police to pursue serial killers and drug traffickers.

These novels flow from Herb's work as a chaplain and mystery devote. He also loves to travel throughout the U.S. But, two of his favorite places to visit are Miami and Key West.

Be sure to read the forthcoming
Death on A1A
Another Perry Savant Novel

www.novelsbyherb.com

www.ingramcontent.com/pod-product-compliance
Lightning Source LLC
Chambersburg PA
CBHW060541180626
46817CB00002B/669